DARK SKIES

A FOX COUNTY FORENSICS LESBIAN ROMANTIC SUSPENSE

CARA MALONE

LISBON PRESS

CONTENT WARNING

This book contains references to sexual assault. There are no on-page depictions or graphic details, but characters discuss an event in which sexual assault occurred. Discretion is advised.

AMELIA

It was a dark and stormy morning...

That was the thought that blew through Dr. Amelia Trace's mind the minute she stepped out of her condo and the wind whipped her blonde hair over her face. It stuck to her tinted lip balm and tangled around the chunky tortoise shell frames of her glasses, and there it would have to stay until she got to her car because she had a lunch bag and briefcase in one hand and a steaming travel mug of coffee in the other.

The skies were eerily dark even though it was only a little past seven-thirty in the morning. Daylight savings time had begun a few weeks ago, so her morning commute was no longer pitch-black—at least on an ordinary day.

This morning, a serious storm was brewing and Amelia just hoped she would get to the office before the skies opened up and all those heavy rain clouds dumped their contents on her. She got to her BMW parked in the driveway and a struggle ensued between her, the door, and the wind. It damn near made off with her coffee mug, but in the end, Amelia prevailed.

She needed that coffee—it was a Monday morning and those tended to be the busiest of the week. She was the chief medical examiner for the county, and her first task of the week was always to check on the cases that had come in over the weekend. Then she would distribute them among herself and the other four pathologists in the office.

If anything happened over the weekend that wouldn't keep until Monday, whoever was on call would have to come in and work, and this weekend it had been Amelia's turn. Of course, with her luck, that meant she'd spent all day Sunday in the morgue working on an apparent homicide victim that had been badly decomposed.

Hence the mug of extra-strong coffee this morning.

On her twenty-minute drive to the office, the mug stayed in its cupholder and Amelia drove with both hands clamped to the wheel as the wind buffeted her car and threatened to shove her out of her lane. It had been a pretty rainy spring so far, but this weather was something else and by the time Amelia pulled into the ME's lot, she was stressed and shaken by the drive. She parked, then sat in the car for a minute, regaining her composure and sipping her coffee in peace before the day began.

"Oh, that's the good stuff," she said, closing her eyes to really savor the creamy hazelnut blend.

She'd allowed her sister Frances to talk her into

buying a fancy Nespresso coffee maker a few weeks ago. Even though she knew Frannie mostly wanted it for when she came to visit, Amelia couldn't deny the appeal now that she had it.

But the wind just kept rocking her car, refusing to let her forget that at any moment a torrential downpour could unleash itself. "Okay, let's do this," she said, gathering her things. She pushed her door open, again with significant resistance, and the wind whipped it shut as soon as she was clear. *Bang.*

And then, nothing.

In an instant, the wind died, the world fell silent, and the hairs on the back of Amelia's neck stood on end.

"Oh shit," she said, seconds before a siren began to wail in the distance. Amelia took off at a run across the parking lot. She lost her grip on her mug—as well as her lunch bag—and left them both where they fell. She reached the medical examiner's office and burst through the door, shouting to her wide-eyed receptionist, "Tornado—get to the basement!"

"Seriously?" the girl, Reese, asked.

Amelia nodded. "Seriously. Go!"

This wasn't the first time in her ten years here that the tornado siren had gone off and she and her staff had to take cover, but it was the first time she'd actually been standing outside and felt the wind die, felt the air crackle with electricity. It felt real, imminent. And it scared the hell out of her.

Fortunately, Reese didn't need telling twice. She got up and bolted through the lobby, heading for the basement, and Amelia called after her, "Take the stairs, not the elevator."

Amelia didn't follow her. As the boss, it was her responsibility to make sure all her employees were safe, even though her pulse was racing so fast she was damn near palpitations. She made a quick circuit through the investigators' cubicles, getting them all to take the siren seriously, and thankfully everyone on the administrative side of the building had already been sufficiently spooked to go downstairs.

Reese must have warned Dylan and Elise, the lab techs, on her way to the basement because their labs were empty. Amelia made sure the morgue was too—at least empty of those with a pulse.

The siren became muted the deeper into the building Amelia went, but she could hear the wind picking up again, reaching a train whistle pitch as she got to the stairwell. Oh God, she thought as she practically flew down the stairs, that's exactly what they say tornados sound like right before they touch down.

"Amelia, in here!" somebody called to her the second her feet touched the concrete floor. A hand hooked around her elbow and her lead investigator, Maya, was pulling her into the women's locker room.

"Is everyone accounted for?" she asked as they rushed past a small row of metal lockers and into the tiled shower area.

"Best we can figure," Maya said. "It's time for a shift change so everybody we know was in the building is down here."

That would just have to be good enough, because in that moment, the overhead lights died and somebody—Reese, maybe?—let out a yelp. Amelia's ears popped as the air pressure spiked, and she crouched in the dark, feeling along the cool tile floor until she found the wall. Then a coworker clutched her hand.

"Hold on, everybody," Amelia said. "It'll be okay."

Ironic words for a woman who dealt with death day in and day out, and investigated cases where people were very much not okay. *It'll be okay* wasn't a promise anyone could actually make.

But sometimes platitudes were all you had to hold on to—that and an anonymous coworker's hand.

2

SIMONE

*I*t was out of the frying pan and into the fire for Lieutenant Simone Olivier and her crew.

She was already at the fire station when the tornado sirens went off. She'd been going over some basic safety procedures with a brand-new batch of three probationary firefighters—probies—and they'd had to drop everything and take cover. The wind whipped up forcefully and shook the solid brick building, but there was no damage to the station when all was said and done.

As much could not be said for the rest of the city.

Simone was tuned into the emergency channel on her radio, and the whole time the wind whistled around the fire station, dispatchers and police officers were calling in downed power lines, injuries and flipped vehicles.

Even the more seasoned members of Simone's crew looked a little overwhelmed—Fox County hadn't had a natural disaster like this for as long as Simone had been a firefighter. But the probies were downright freaked.

"I can't believe this is happening on my first day," one of them, Larson, said when the danger passed and he crawled out of the fetal position.

"Lucky you—trial by fire," Simone's best friend at the station, Carter, said. He always took great joy in teasing a new batch of probies, but as the station lieutenant, Simone was the one who actually had to deal with them. And today she had to deal with three recruits and a city on fire.

"Shut it, Carter," she said. He made a crude but playful gesture, and Simone waved her crew out of the hallway where they'd taken shelter. "Come on, everybody, we've got work to do."

She could tell from the chatter on the emergency channel that there would be fires to put out, both literally and figuratively. The five regular day shift crew members, Simone included, and her three probies headed upstairs where she told them all to suit up.

They started to walk toward the fire engine and she clapped her hands, shouting, "Come on, get the lead out!"

The three probies—Larson, Velez and Williams—broke into a run and Simone kept an eye on them. They were slow, more concerned with putting everything on in the right order than with getting out the door. There'd be plenty of time to adjust clothing while they were on the rig.

When there wasn't a natural disaster to deal with, she'd have to run drills with them to get it right.

Just then, the station alarm started to wail. They were getting a call, and now it really was a matter of urgency.

Simone's four vets all hopped onto the fire engine. They didn't need to be told twice, but the probies were still struggling with their gear. Simone herded them toward the vehicle. "Go, go, you can fix it on the way."

"I think I'm gonna puke," Williams complained as he boarded the fire engine.

"You can do it on the way," Simone said, and then they were out the door, sirens blaring.

Williams did look a little clammy, as did Larson. Simone couldn't blame them for being nervous on their first day, let alone a first day that had started like this one. But every time she looked at Velez, the only female among the new recruits, she was stone-faced and determined. Maybe she was freaking out on the inside just like the other two, but if she was, she was fighting like hell not to show it.

You couldn't when you were a female doing a job like this, with so much testosterone and macho energy all around. The men all gave each other shit any time they showed weakness on the job. For a female firefighter to be perceived as weak... it was career suicide.

By the time the fire engine came to a stop in a residential neighborhood about five minutes away from the station, Simone had a burgeoning respect for Velez and high hopes that she'd do well in this job. Larson and

Williams would probably be fine too, but they didn't remind Simone of her younger self the way Velez did.

At least nobody had upchucked.

"Okay, everybody out," Simone said, mostly for the benefit of the probies. Her regular crew knew the drill—they rarely needed her to direct them.

Simone had been talking to dispatch on her radio the whole way over so she knew there was one active fire, and several houses in the neighborhood had been torn apart, so there would be search-and-rescue work to do. Her probies were definitely not ready for it—Simone would put Carter in charge of that.

As soon as she stepped off the fire engine, the extent of the destruction took her breath away.

This was more than high winds. The tornado had come right through sleepy suburban Balch Street, not just damaging but leveling four houses. The ones that were still standing were almost untouched—a few shingles ripped off here, a piece of siding missing there. And yet their neighbors' houses had ceased to exist.

"Holy shit," Larson said as everyone took in the scene. He pointed to one of the downed houses. "Those people have to be wondering what they did to piss off God."

"Those people could be dead," Simone snapped, glaring so hard he actually shrank inside his fire-resistant jacket. Good, he wouldn't make the mistake of voicing snarky, insensitive comments like that again.

She barked out orders, making sure everyone knew what they were doing. She sent the experienced crew to liaise with the police who were arriving on the scene to coordinate the search-and-rescue efforts. Then she let the probies fight their first fire.

They pulled heavy reels of fire hoses off the vehicle while Simone checked out the burning house and made sure the gas running in from the street had been shut off. The house was still mostly standing, but black smoke was billowing from a broken downstairs window, and if they didn't act fast, it wouldn't be standing for long.

"Over here," she called to her three recruits.

Velez led the way with Larson trailing behind her, carrying the slack of the fire hose, and Williams ran over to a hydrant nearby. At least that hadn't been touched by the tornado. Simone jogged over to join him, showing him how to connect the hose and turn on the water with a special hydrant wrench.

"Aim low, keep the hose under control," she instructed.

While the probies tackled the fire, Simone had one eye on them and one on the rest of the neighborhood. It was still eerily dark for a spring morning, and the sky looked like it could open up and downpour again at any moment. There were at least a half-dozen police cars here, with more arriving all the time. This neighborhood must have been one of the worst hit by the tornado.

Simone kept scanning while she supervised, but she didn't see any people—dead or alive—being pulled out of the wrecked houses. Maybe that meant there weren't any casualties. Maybe they'd all left for work already and that would be the silver lining.

Fingers crossed.

"Good," she told Velez, pointing. "Keep spraying. We want to put this fire out before it has a chance to spread to the rest of these houses."

It was a small fire and Simone felt confident that even a crew of complete newbies could handle it, but that didn't make the situation any less serious. This whole neighborhood was a tinderbox and the last thing she wanted was to lose the last standing houses to fire after the tornado took out the rest of the neighborhood.

"Incoming," she heard Carter call.

She looked up the road, where he was directing traffic as the medical examiner's distinctive white van crept through the debris and the haphazardly parked emergency vehicles on the road.

"Shit," Simone muttered. There was only one reason for the ME to be here—there were casualties after all.

3

AMELIA

*T*he scene was like something out of a war zone. Houses had been destroyed seemingly at random, others nearly untouched, and there was a fire burning in one that was still standing.

Amelia had been a forensic pathologist for ten years, the chief medical examiner for the last three, so she'd seen her fair share of horrible stuff. That didn't mean it got any easier, though, and as she climbed out of the van, it occurred to her that she should be grateful for that fact. It meant she hadn't lost her humanity, hadn't gotten jaded from the job.

She went around to the back of the van to retrieve an investigation kit. It felt heavy and a little foreign in her hands—her work was mostly done back at the ME's office. It was rare that she actually came out to a scene, but today it was all hands on deck. Before she left the office, she'd called in every single one of her investigators and activated the office's mass fatality protocol.

And now it was time to get to work.

"Where do you want me, doc?" Kelsey Granger asked, picking up her own investigation kit.

She was one of the more junior investigators and usually worked the night shift. She was going to med school during the day, working on becoming a forensic pathologist herself, and though Amelia's path didn't cross with Kelsey's often because of their opposing schedules, she'd offered to mentor her once she got to the hands-on portion of her studies.

Given the destruction in just this one neighborhood, Amelia knew all her investigators would be working overtime for a while and Kelsey would likely be missing a lot of class.

"Stick with me for now," Amelia told her. "I want to get the lay of the land and come up with a game plan before we split up."

Kelsey nodded, then closed the van doors.

They walked slowly up the street, stepping over sticks and bits of debris flung off the houses, and Amelia warned Kelsey to look out for nails. The last thing she needed was an investigator out of commission due to tetanus.

Amelia spotted the chief of police, and that was how she knew this was the worst-hit neighborhood in the city. She and Kelsey picked their way over to him. He was talking to a couple of cops, directing them to turn off the gas to the rest of the houses on the street.

"Chief Wilson," Amelia said when the officers left,

"how's the rest of the city looking? Hopefully not as bad as this?"

Wilson let out a huff of air. "Wish I could say so, but Lakeland Avenue got hit pretty hard too. Lot of fatalities going to be coming your way today. You ready for it?"

"The mass disaster protocol has been activated," Amelia said. She'd dispatched a handful of her investigators to Lakeland Avenue based on the information she got from the police dispatchers, and more calls were coming in from around the city. It was only nine a.m. and there were already more scenes than investigators, so she'd have to reassign them as they became available. For now, though, she needed to get a handle on this scene. "I was going to set up a grid and start working through this neighborhood with Ms. Granger, unless you have anything that needs my attention first?"

The chief shook his head. "I hope we find survivors here, but I'm afraid this is more your scene than mine."

She nodded. That meant they hadn't had much luck with search-and-rescue so far.

"Come on," she said to Kelsey, "let's find the fire captain and find out which of these houses are safe to enter."

---

*H*alf an hour later, the initial scene assessment was done, their grid was established, and Amelia and Kelsey had split up to begin their work.

There was *some* good news. A handful of survivors had been pulled from their homes and were clustered around the ambulances parked at one end of the street, getting medical care for minor cuts and bruises.

But there was also a growing list of victims. Firefighters and police officers told Amelia and Kelsey where there were bodies that they'd located, and Amelia recorded their locations according to the grid. It was Amelia and Kelsey's job to document and remove each body.

Hopefully there wouldn't be any additional surprises, but there were already too many bodies to transport in the van. Amelia called to order one of the refrigerated trucks she'd had on standby since activating the mass disaster protocol, then she got to work.

Amelia started at one end of the street and Kelsey went to the other. Her first set of victims was an elderly couple in a half-demolished home who hadn't managed to get to their basement before the tornado touched down. The woman had been struck by flying debris and the man appeared to be dead of a heart attack. They were the first fatalities that the police had discovered upon arrival, which had prompted them to call the ME's office.

Amelia took photos and applied ID tags to the decedents' toes—Jane and John Doe, until the police could match up the location of their bodies with the residents of the house and make a positive identification. She called a couple firefighters over to help her lift them out of the house and place them in body bags, then laid them in the shade until the refrigerated truck arrived.

She was finishing her documentation of them when she heard a low, unhappy whining that reminded her of Frannie's Dachshund. She went carefully back into the house and followed the sound to a bedroom.

"Hey, there," she announced herself. "It's okay, I'm here to help."

She looked around for the source of the noise, musing while she did that for the second time in a couple of hours, she'd promised that everything was okay when it definitely wasn't.

She crouched down and found a terrified but otherwise unharmed beagle under the bed. "Hi, baby. You gotta come here now, okay?"

His humans were gone, and Amelia found her vision misting over. How many fatality cases had she worked on in the past decade? And yet animals never failed to tug on her heartstrings. She could never be a veterinarian or she'd cry every day.

It was a challenge to get the beagle out from its hiding spot, but finally she managed. She quickly wiped her cheeks on her sleeve, then carried it out of the house and passed it off to the nearest cop she saw. "Found this little guy in there," she told the cop. "Owners are dead—see if you can find next of kin to look after him?"

"Umm, sure," the cop said, looking uncertain.

Amelia didn't wait around to find out the dog's fate. There were a lot of people who needed her, even if they were dead. Plus, her walkie-talkie crackled to life and Kelsey told her that she'd found more remains.

"Got a Caucasian male, looks around fifty years of age," she said. "Puncture wound to the chest due to debris."

Another one. Amelia shook her head, trying not to let the quickly increasing body count get to her. Sometimes, rarely, she had to dissociate from a scene and start viewing the decedents as objects to be examined rather than human beings. She thought she would be okay today, but that damn orphaned dog had gotten to her.

Now, as she responded to Kelsey then continued to the next victim on her list, she thought about how arbitrary death could be.

All these people were just living their lives a few hours ago, completely oblivious to the fact that they would soon be over. Amelia herself had started her day worrying about the entirely trivial possibility of getting wet on her way to work—

An impossibly young firefighter whipped around the corner of a house and slammed into Amelia so hard it knocked the wind out of her, to say nothing of disrupting her thoughts.

"Oops, sorry!" he said, then continued on his way.

Amelia took another step and two more firefighters came around the corner. This time she flattened herself against the house to avoid being bulldozed.

Then, just as she was peeling herself off the wall, a fourth one appeared, calmer and more controlled. She looked older than the other three, but probably about ten years younger than Amelia, in her early thirties by the looks of it. And she had the most gorgeous hazel eyes and a delicate, upturned nose.

She brushed her gloved hand over Amelia's arm as she gracefully avoided the collision.

"Excuse me," she said, her voice low and velvety.

"That's okay," Amelia said. "But how many more of you are there? Maybe I should find another way around."

"Did my probies nearly run into you too?" the woman asked.

Amelia smiled. "Two of them were near-collisions. The first one totaled me."

"You don't look totaled to me," the woman said, her eyes momentarily flitting down to Amelia's lips. The look sent an unexpected thrill through her. Then the spell was broken as, suddenly, the woman leaned around Amelia's shoulder and shouted, "Larson! Did you crash into the ME?"

Amelia glanced behind herself, where the three young firefighters were standing together. The kid who'd hit-and-run on her had a sheepish look on his face.

"Sorry," he said. "I was in a rush."

"We all are," the woman said. "Let's try not to create any more injuries than the tornado already has."

He gave her a hangdog look, then she turned back to Amelia. "Sorry. It's their first day and they're practically feral."

Amelia laughed. "It's not that big a deal."

Then she caught herself smiling and got serious again. For a second, she'd forgotten her surroundings, forgotten the enormity of the situation and how many lives had been lost, how many homes destroyed. When was the last time a woman had that much power over her, and all within thirty seconds of meeting?

The woman took her glove off and held out her hand. "Lieutenant Simone Olivier."

Her name was like a song, exotic and beautiful, and Amelia felt a spark as she took Simone's hand.

Simone's lips curled into a wry smile when she felt it too.

"Sorry, these damn gloves," she said, but Amelia was pretty sure that static electricity only accounted for a small portion of what she'd just felt.

She cleared her throat, realizing she hadn't introduced herself yet. "I'm Dr. Amelia Trace."

"I know," Simone said, that smile still on her lips like there was a secret only the two of them knew. Amelia could feel it in her belly, her core growing hot the longer she looked into those wide, warm eyes.

Stop, she begged herself.

Then Simone's fingers slid out of Amelia's and she worked her hand back into her glove.

"Gotta go corral the puppies before they get up to dickens," she said, and then she was gone and Amelia temporarily forgot what the heck she'd been doing, where the hell she was going.

She permitted herself just a few seconds longer to watch Simone rallying her recruits and coordinating them. They were searching the structurally sound houses. Amelia had a surprisingly difficult time tearing her eyes away from Simone.

She hadn't woken up today expecting a mass disaster, but at least she had a plan in place for that. There were binders and resource lists and annual trainings for that. But the gorgeous, subtly flirtatious firefighter she'd just met? Amelia had no contingency plan for Simone.

4

SIMONE

"Hey, I've got more survivors over here!" Carter called.

Simone's attention immediately snapped away from the ME, who she'd been watching out of the corner of her eye. She and the probies were shoring up a partially downed wall to make sure none of the first responders got hurt, but she pulled them away from it now.

"Go, go," she ordered, pointing them to the house Carter had shouted from. "All hands on deck."

The four of them ran across the street, along with everyone else within earshot. That included Dr. Amelia Trace, but for the moment, Simone had to shut Amelia and her golden hair out of her head. They had pressing work to do.

"What have we got?" she asked Carter.

The faint shouts coming from deep within the house were answer enough. There had to be at least five voices, maybe more, and shit, they sounded young.

"I was testing the structure when I heard them," Carter said. "Tornado ripped away the whole north side of the house—we've got to get them out fast before the rest of it comes down."

"Okay," Simone said, her mind racing. She ran through a quick mental list of all the things they needed to do, then she started barking orders. Everything happened in a high-adrenaline blur, and the probies seemed to sense the importance of the task because they actually did as she asked without question or screw-up.

Maybe they had some potential after all.

It took about ten minutes to temporarily support the house, then clear a path to the partially obliterated basement stairs. It was a risk—the whole structure was compromised and even with the additional support, it could collapse any minute. But there were civilians down there and this was what firefighters did—they put the community ahead of themselves.

When the first survivor emerged from the basement, his arm slung over Carter's shoulder for support, Simone shouted, "We need medics over here!"

There were already a few standing by and they sprang into action.

Simone's crew pulled five teenage boys out of the basement, along with a woman who said she was the mother of one of them. All six had escaped fatal injury, but a couple of them had pretty serious wounds. Not everyone in the house had been so lucky, though.

"We need the ME," Simone said when she emerged from the basement with Velez, carrying the first corpse between them. This time she wasn't nearly so loud, resignation weighing down her voice.

The victim was another teenaged boy, and one of the survivors let out a strangled cry when he spotted him.

"Henry," he said, and the paramedics had to wrestle him back onto the back of their ambulance so they could continue treating a deep cut on his leg.

"What should we do with... Henry?" Velez asked Simone. She was carrying his feet while Simone held the dead boy beneath his arms.

"Lay him on the ground and cover him," Amelia instructed.

"Far enough away from the house in case it collapses," Simone added, nodding where she wanted Velez to walk.

Her crew pulled another teenage boy out of the house—they were both dead from apparent crushing injuries, and Dr. Trace began documenting the scene.

"We found them both under a collapsed pool table," Simone told her. "Looked like they were trying to seek shelter, but those tables are heavy."

The adult woman, standing near the boy with the leg injury, started sobbing. "Noah was having a sleepover, you know, to celebrate the start of summer vacation. And now those boys are dead... because of *my* pool table..."

"Because of the tornado, ma'am," Simone said. "This isn't your fault."

"Elizabeth, please," she said. "Ma'am was my mother."

Her attempt at humor fell flat, just like the words

themselves. She was running on autopilot and was probably in shock. She didn't appear to be wounded, but just to be safe, she would doubtless get checked out by the medics.

"Is he your son?" Simone asked, nodding to the boy in the ambulance.

Elizabeth nodded. "Noah." Then she pointed to the two dead boys. "That's Henry Felton, and Riley Poole. Oh God, who's going to tell their parents?"

"An officer will do that," Simone assured her.

Then Noah sat up taller, on full alert and once again disrupting the paramedics' attempts to stop the bleeding on his leg. "Wait, who's that?"

Everybody's eyes went back to the house, where Larson and Williams were carrying out another body. This one was female, also young.

Elizabeth furrowed her brow. "I have no idea."

"She wasn't with you in the house?" Simone asked.

Elizabeth shook her head. "It was just me and the boys. Noah and his friends. My husband had already left for work when the siren sounded."

Simone looked around at the surviving teenagers. Besides Noah, one other boy was receiving medical treatment, and the other three sat on the grass, looking shaken. They didn't look guilty, but Simone asked, just to be sure, "None of you snuck a girl into the house?"

They all shook their heads, and Elizabeth answered for them. "They're good boys."

Noah added, "I've never seen that girl before."

"Maybe she was in the neighborhood when the

tornado hit," Velez suggested. "She could have been seeking shelter and yours was the nearest house."

"I don't see how that's possible," Elizabeth said. "This is a safe neighborhood, but we always lock our doors."

"You're sure you found her in the basement?" Amelia asked Williams and Larson. It *was* a little hard to tell, with half of the first floor in shambles.

But they nodded, confident. "Yeah, with the others."

Well, it wasn't like the middle of a tornado was a calm place to be, where you had plenty of time to observe your surroundings. Anything could have happened while Elizabeth and the boys were seeking shelter in the basement. Maybe the girl broke a window to get in—it wasn't like anyone would be able to tell now.

"We've got to take him to the hospital now," one of the paramedics said, gesturing to Noah. "He needs stitches, and probably some blood."

"I'm going with you," Elizabeth said, already climbing into the ambulance.

"I'm fine, Mom," Noah tried to reassure her, but she gave him a stern look.

"You're not fine. Didn't you just hear that man say you need stitches?"

The kid managed to roll his eyes for the benefit of his friends in true teenager fashion, then somebody pulled the door shut and the engine started. At most other scenes, the ambulance would be out of here by now, maybe even with the sirens wailing. But the road had only been partially cleared of debris, so both ambulances formed a slow-moving caravan picking their way carefully through the neighborhood.

The police gathered the three uninjured boys and took them away to reunite them with their parents.

Then Simone turned to Amelia. "So, what happens next for them?"

She gestured to the three bodies they'd pulled out of the house. It was an unfortunate reality of the job that she'd encountered her fair share of bodies, but she wasn't used to sticking around. Firefighters were usually the first in and the first out, always moving on to the next emergency. But today was different.

Today, everybody was a little lost, just trying to be useful.

"I called for a refrigerated truck when I saw how many bodies there were," Amelia said. "It should be arriving any minute."

A chill ran up the back of Simone's neck, setting the fine hairs on end. It was the same feeling she got whenever she heard an emergency siren—an injection of adrenaline and déjà vu that brought her back to all the people she hadn't been able to help over the course of her career.

She shoved it aside as always and asked, "That bad, huh?"

Amelia nodded. "We could only transport one at a time in the van anyway, but we only typically have around twenty cases at a time. This neighborhood's casualties alone would stress our resources, and then you have to add in all the other areas of the city that have been affected."

"Depressing," Simone said.

"Sorry," Amelia answered.

Simone shrugged. "Nobody's fault. It's just a shitty day is all."

Still, she didn't envy the medical examiner's job. Running into a burning building to rescue someone was one thing. All you had to do was turn off the part of your brain responsible for self-preservation and do whatever it took to make the save. Cataloging, identifying and autopsying enough bodies that a refrigerated truck is necessary, on the other hand... Simone had no clue what part of your brain you had to turn off to get through something like that.

One thing was for sure—Amelia Trace was one badass woman if she could handle that.

"Oh my God, my house!"

They were interrupted by a man sprinting up the sidewalk, making a beeline for them.

"Sir, you can't go in there," Simone said. "It isn't safe."

"My wife!" he shouted. "My son! They were home, I've been trying to call and I can't get through. This damn neighborhood always has had shit reception!"

"A lot of phone lines are down around the city right now," a nearby cop interjected. "And the cell towers are jammed because everybody's trying to call their loved ones."

"Elizabeth and Noah are okay," Simone told the man.

She practically had to tackle him to keep him from running into the half-destroyed home. "What's your name?"

He looked annoyed at the diversion, but spit his name out on autopilot. "Cal. Calvin Thomas."

"Cal, your son was injured and he needs stitches and probably a transfusion, but he'll be fine," Simone assured him. "Your wife is unharmed. She's with your son on the way to the hospital now."

"I'm a universal donor, I can help," he was saying, but then he got distracted when his eyes fell on the three bodies that had been pulled from his house. "Oh my God."

Simone was grateful that her probies had at least done as she said and covered the bodies. "A couple of your son's friends didn't make it," she said, softening her voice. She looked to Amelia for help, but it wasn't like either of them spent a lot of their time comforting survivors.

Dr. Trace stepped forward. She put a hand on the man's shoulder in a comforting gesture and said, "Sir, the police may have questions for your wife and son, and maybe you too."

"Questions?" Cal asked, bewildered.

"But for right now, you should just go be with them," Amelia told him. "They didn't leave long before you arrived—if you go now, you might catch up before they get to the hospital."

"Just be careful of debris," Simone added.

Cal Thomas headed back toward his car, and Amelia asked, "Do you think he's okay to drive?"

"I hope so," Simone said. "We don't need any more emergencies right now." She looked back to the bodies not far from them. "You didn't want to show him the girl, see if he could identify her, Dr. Trace?"

"Call me Amelia," she said, a smile forming momentarily on her lips. Then she shook her head. "He's got enough on his plate right now, and so do we. Plus, that's a job for the police."

They watched as a big white eighteen-wheeler crunched its way slowly into the neighborhood, then let out the air brake.

"Refrigerated truck's here," Amelia said.

"Oh God," Simone breathed. She'd been picturing something so much smaller, like one of those little U-Hauls people rented when they didn't actually have that much stuff to move. This was just grim.

"I know," Amelia said, reading her mind. Then she put her hand on Simone's shoulder. It was the same comforting gesture she'd used on Cal Thomas a few minutes ago, but this time she lingered for a moment. It felt more personal, less clinical. And Simone was ashamed to admit it turned her on a little, even out here in this macabre setting. "We'll get through this."

"Do you want help?" she asked when Amelia's hand trailed away. "Moving the bodies, I mean?"

"Only if you're not busy," she said. "I still need to photograph them first."

"I don't mind," Simone said. "I'm yours as long as nobody on my crew needs me."

It took more than an hour to photograph the bodies—Amelia did it right there in the grass since it wasn't possible to document them where they were found. Then Simone helped her tag them, and at last they were ready to be zipped into body bags and moved to the refrigerated truck.

Or trailer, more accurately.

These three were the first to go in, and Simone prayed she wouldn't have to see what it looked like when the trailer was full.

When they got to the girl, they laid a body bag out beside her and Simone lifted her feet. Amelia went to the girl's head, but she didn't lift her. "Wait."

"What's wrong?"

Instead of answering, Amelia looked around for her investigation kit. She found it and pulled out a pair of tweezers and a small plastic evidence bag. Then she knelt in front of the body, scrutinizing the girl's upper arm.

"What is it?" Simone asked, looking over her shoulder.

"There's a wound here, and I think I saw a glint of metal," Amelia said, deep in concentration. She set the evidence bag down on top of the body bag, then probed a wound in the girl's upper arm with the tweezers. A little bit of dark, coagulating blood oozed out, and then Amelia produced the snub-nosed slug of a small-caliber bullet.

Simone grabbed the evidence bag and held it open for Amelia. "She was shot?"

"I assumed this was a puncture wound when I first saw it," she explained. "Not at all uncommon when there's flying debris everywhere. I wouldn't have discovered the bullet until X-rays were done if it hadn't caught the light just right."

She and Simone both looked into the sky. That light almost had to be some kind of divine intervention because it was still overcast, the clouds heavy with rain. The sun was peeking through a small break in the cloud cover, but it wouldn't last long.

"So what does this mean?" Simone asked. "Homicide?"

"I don't know," Amelia said. "A bullet wound in that location probably isn't the cause of death, but it does raise a lot more questions. Based on the amount of blood, I'd say she was shot very near the time of death, and yet nobody in that house knew she was there. None of them heard a gunshot?"

"Tornados can be pretty loud," Simone pointed out.

"True," Amelia answered. "Come on, help me finish this up—looks like it's going to rain again any minute and I don't want any evidence to get washed away."

They worked together to lift the girl into the body bag, and then Amelia tucked the small evidence bag inside it too. Then they carried her to the refrigerated truck.

As they went, Amelia looked lost in thought. They laid the girl down with the others, then walked back down the ramp to the ground.

"One thing's for certain," Amelia said at last. "We're

going to have to investigate that house much more thoroughly."

"Today?" Simone asked, concern rippling through her at the idea of Amelia going inside that death trap. "It's not safe—"

"Hey, look out!"

Somebody shouted and everyone within earshot reflexively crouched, covering their heads. Simone heard the distinctive crack of lumber splitting, something she'd heard hundreds of times on the job, and she looked around to see which house was giving up the ghost.

"Oh no!" Amelia said, and Simone knew.

They stood there at the opening to the refrigerated truck, cold air at their backs and rain droplets beginning to wet their hair. And they watched Elizabeth and Noah's house crumble further.

One of the remaining exterior walls crumbled, the bricks at the bottom nearly disintegrating as they fell into the yard right where the bodies had been laid. Right where Amelia and Simone had been working just a few minutes ago.

"Oh shit," Simone said, grabbing Amelia's hand and pulling her around the side of the truck just to be safe. They stepped behind it as a big plume of dirt and dust billowed out of the wreckage, and after everything settled, they hazarded a peek.

The danger seemed to have passed, and Simone stepped out from behind the trailer, asking into her radio, "Everybody okay?"

There was a volley of responses from her firefighters,

all checking in with her. Then she turned back to Amelia.

"You okay?"

"Well, the investigation just got a bit more complicated," she said. "Do you think it'll collapse any further?"

"Probably," Simone said. She was no building engineer, but she'd never seen a house missing two walls where the roof didn't also come down. "You can't go in there again today, but I'll see what my crew can do about making it safe."

"Thank you," she said. "I'm glad I ran into you today."

Simone gave her a wry smile. "Me too."

"In any case, there's nothing left that can go wrong today," Amelia said.

And with that, a crack of lightning lit up the sky.

5

AMELIA

The sky opened up as if a dam had been breached. Amelia and Simone were drenched within seconds, and everyone around them was running for cover.

Amelia didn't have that luxury, though. As soon as she found that bullet wound in her Jane Doe, the house where she'd been discovered had become a crime scene. One that had, unfortunately, just partially collapsed... but that didn't mean there wasn't still evidence to be found there.

Evidence that could easily wash away in a downpour like this.

She took off at a mad dash toward the white Medical Examiner's van parked at the other end of the neighborhood. She wasn't entirely sure what she was looking for—some tarps to cover what she could, or maybe just Kelsey, an extra set of experienced hands. This wasn't a typical death scene, and everything they did today was guesswork.

When she got to the van, Kelsey was nowhere in sight. She was probably sheltering from the rain like everyone else.

Amelia flung open the back doors and hopped in, and she nearly screamed when somebody jumped in after her. Then she noticed it was Simone.

"What are you doing?" she asked. She practically had to shout over the sound of the rain pelting the metal roof of the van.

"I've been asking you the same thing!" Simone shouted back. "I was calling your name but you didn't stop."

"I didn't hear you," Amelia explained. "I'm trying to find something to cover the crime scene, help preserve evidence."

There were cabinets on both walls of the van, filled with all kinds of supplies for pretty much any eventuality. Anything except a house torn in half by a tornado. Still, she opened a few, looked around—just in case.

"Do you have a tarp big enough to cover a two-story house?" Simone shouted over the storm.

Amelia stopped looking. It *was* a pretty ridiculous thing to expect to find in the ME van, and even if she *did* find one, was she going to scale one of the remaining walls to cover the house? Hell no.

She sat down on the steel gurney taking up the center of the van, the one they used to transport the deceased under normal circumstances. "Okay, I see your point."

Suddenly, she was feeling red in the face. What was the chief medical examiner doing freaking out and losing her senses? She was supposed to be cool, calm and collected—her team needed that from her.

Simone sat down beside her and nodded at the rain beyond the van doors. "We might as well take a breather. There's nothing we can do right now."

Amelia nodded, and Simone used her radio to let her crew know where she was in case they needed her. There was a moment of silence once she finished, and it actually felt peaceful for the first time all morning.

The steady drum of the rain reminded Amelia of quiet summer nights, lying in bed with a window above her head, listening to rain tapping the glass. It reminded her of one particular night a long time ago, when she was in middle school.

Her best friend, Sam, was sleeping over, and they'd decided to share Amelia's bed. Frannie was just a few feet away in a bed on the other side of the room, and Amelia's heart was pounding so hard because she'd dreamed about curling up with Sam for so long. Rain pattered on the window above her headboard and she was sure she wouldn't get any sleep at all that night. And then, Sam's hand had found hers beneath the covers.

Rain had always been romantic to Amelia, ever since that night.

And now she was sitting on a gurney used to transport the dead, inside a van in the middle of a disaster area, with a woman she just met. This should have been the least romantic setting ever conceived, and yet Amelia found her hand itching to reach out to Simone's.

Instead, she decided to go the self-deprecation route.

"Sorry I freaked out and made you chase me through the rain," she said. "I know I'm supposed to be in control, being the boss and all. But this is my first mass disaster and it's stressful."

Simone was a fire lieutenant. She probably never panicked. She probably had nerves of steel, which only made Amelia feel worse about her irrational dash through the rain.

"I hope it's your only mass disaster," Simone said, then gave her a sympathetic smile. "It's my first too."

"And yet you're weathering it so much better," Amelia said, feeling the heat rising in her cheeks. Or maybe it was the humidity quickly building in the van thanks to the rain.

"I wouldn't say that," she answered. "Did you see me cursing out my recruits for going into a house that hadn't been cleared?"

Amelia smiled. "No, I missed that."

"Good, it wasn't pretty," Simone answered. She smiled broadly, openly. She had perfect teeth and exact symmetry in her features, but what was even more attractive to Amelia was the way she wore her heart on her sleeve and how she seemed completely comfortable around Amelia right from the start.

"I'm sure it was," Amelia said, surprising herself. Was she flirting on the job? On the most critical day of her career thus far? Who was this person inhabiting her body?

"Everybody needs to let off steam once in a while," Simone continued. "You apparently needed to run through the rain."

Amelia smiled, slicking back her hair when she felt a trickle starting on her forehead. "I really am soaking wet. So are you... sorry."

"I'd never ask a pretty lady to apologize for making me wet," Simone said.

Oh holy shit... well, that removed all doubt about those looks Simone had been giving her, her motivations for following Amelia through the rain, what they were doing on this gurney together. For a second, Amelia couldn't breathe. For a second, she considered kissing Simone right then and there.

And then the rain stopped as abruptly as it had started. It was so fast that the absence of drumming on the roof was almost a sound of its own.

They both looked toward the open van doors and Simone said, "I hope this isn't the eye of the storm."

Then someone opened the driver door behind them and Amelia nearly screamed again. Guilt at what she'd just been thinking washed over her. She swallowed it down and turned. "Kelsey."

"Oh, Dr. Trace," she said, looking equally surprised to see the two of them. "I didn't know you were here."

"Just getting in from the rain," Simone said, then reached between the seats to introduce herself. "Lieutenant Olivier."

"Kelsey Granger," she answered. "I was thinking it'd be nice to move the van closer to the refrigerated truck in case we need supplies. Is that okay, Dr. Trace?"

"Sure," she said. "Let's just pull the doors closed or we'll lose everything on the way over."

She and Simone did so, then sat back down on the gurney. The trip was bumpy because the most recent rain storm had brought down even more branches and blown house debris across the road again. Amelia gripped the edge of the gurney to stabilize herself, and her pinky finger curled over Simone's.

"Sorry," she said softly, quickly pulling her hand away.

"Don't be," Simone answered.

Then Kelsey asked from the front seat, "How's it going for you, Dr. Trace? I've been so busy I've hardly seen you."

Amelia switched back into boss mode, forcefully shutting down any feelings that had been rising to the surface when it came to Simone. She gave Kelsey a run-down of the three victims the firefighters had pulled from the Thomas house, and the bullet wound she'd discovered in Jane Doe.

"Cause of death?" Kelsey asked.

"No," Amelia said. "Quite possibly perimortem, though." That meant it had occurred at the time of death, or shortly before.

"Interesting," Kelsey said, pondering the case as she parked the van next to the eighteen-wheeler.

"Agreed," Amelia answered, still mulling over what

she knew so far. It wasn't much, but it definitely didn't add up to a natural death.

"I'm available to help you now," Kelsey said. "Some of the firefighters and I canvassed the neighborhood and we're confident there are no more victims."

"How many have there been?" Simone asked.

"The team I was working with found three," Kelsey said.

"So that makes six total, just on this street," Simone said, shaking her head.

"Sounds like we have our work cut out for us," Amelia said. "Come on, Kelsey, you can help me investigate the Thomas house... or what's left of it."

"I'll keep you both safe," Simone said. "Or, as safe as possible."

Amelia opened the back door and jumped out, aware that Simone was following on her heels. She liked having her around, but at the same time, she didn't trust herself to act entirely professional now that Kelsey was around to observe them.

There was just something about Simone that made all her hard-won professionalism go right out the proverbial window.

6

SIMONE

*S*imone pulled in a couple of her seasoned crew members to help secure the remaining structure of the house. While they worked, Amelia kept her distance, photographing the exterior and avoiding Simone's eye.

Was she imagining it, or was Amelia ignoring her like a kid with a crush who couldn't trust her emotions in the presence of an audience? It was sort of cute.

Simone tried to focus—what she was doing was important to make sure no one else got hurt—but her mind kept drifting back to being alone in the ME van with Amelia. Things had gotten steamy, literally and figuratively, and she wondered if something good could come of this awful day. Maybe before it was all done, she could get Amelia's number, take her out to dinner and see what she was like when she wasn't drenched, wearing PPE and moving bodies around.

She'd have to be hotter by at least a factor of ten,

right? And she was already one of the most stunning women Simone had ever encountered.

Simone guessed they had an age difference of about a decade, and she always did have a thing for older women. With her thick-framed glasses and her blonde hair pulled back in a practical ponytail, Amelia had a sort of mature Gillian Anderson vibe going on. And that just so happened to be a vibe Simone was powerless to resist.

She and Carter did their best shoring up the house, then she realized she hadn't heard from the probies since before the downpour. Lord knew what they were up to.

Simone jogged over to Amelia, who was absorbed in photographing the wreckage.

"Hey, I need to check on my recruits," she told her. "Carter and I did what we could here, but promise me you won't go into that house without help."

Amelia looked up from her camera, that spark in her eyes again. "Do I look like a woman who needs help?"

"No," Simone admitted, "but you do look like a human who's vulnerable to crushing injuries if there's another collapse."

Amelia smiled wryly. "Point taken."

"I'll be right back," Simone promised.

"Bring your recruits, if they're not busy," Amelia said. "We can use all the help we can get to process this scene quickly and minimize the risk."

"Sure thing," Simone said. She wandered through the neighborhood and, before long, found her three probies working with a police officer to clear the debris on the road. "Hey, how's it going?"

"Good," Velez said. "We cordoned off that downed power line."

She pointed to a black cable running across someone's yard, yellow caution tape strung up all around it. Simone asked, "Is it live?"

Velez nodded. "We notified the power company."

"Guy I talked to was a complete dick," the cop grumbled. "Acted like I was demanding special treatment or something. He said there are a ton of lines down around the city."

"Yeah, I can imagine," Simone said. "I don't know an F5 tornado from a Dyson vacuum, but I can tell just from this neighborhood that it was a severe storm. Did he give any indication how long the wait will be?"

The cop shook his head. "He just said he'd add Balch Street to the list."

"Great," Simone said, rolling her eyes. "Well, if you can spare these three, Dr. Trace asked for a few volunteers to help her with her crime scene."

"Crime scene?" Williams asked. "I thought this was a natural disaster."

"It's both, apparently," Simone said. While they walked over to the Thomas house, Simone told them about the mystery woman and the gunshot wound Amelia had discovered on her arm.

When they arrived, an unmarked black SUV was parked in front of the house and a detective Simone recognized was standing on the lawn, talking to Amelia.

"Tom Logan," Simone called, then gestured to the SUV. "What happened, did you wreck your Town Car?"

"Nah, I got an upgrade—chief said all the senior detectives are getting them eventually, but I think it's compensation for taking a bullet on the job," he said, pointing to his thigh.

Simone had heard about his last case. When the police chief's daughter apprehends a perp, the news tends to travel fast, and Tom—who'd gotten caught in the crossfire—wound up sounding like the damsel in distress in that particular situation. He still favored his injured leg when he walked, but at least he'd gotten a nicer vehicle out of the ordeal.

"Well, you look like you're nearly back to your usual horrible self," Simone said with a grin. "Are you working this case?"

He nodded, and Amelia said, "I filled him in on what we know so far."

"Well, I've got a gaggle of brand-new probies at your disposal," Simone said. "What can we do to help?"

Tom was more than happy to have a few extra hands at his disposal, especially since he wasn't as ambulatory as he once was. "The house is a mess and I don't think I'm up to crawling through the wreckage. I take it no one handed over the gun?"

Amelia shook her head. "Three of the survivors are at the hospital now, and the others went home to their parents. They all left before we discovered the gunshot wound, and none of them knew the victim."

"Yeah, that's what they always say," Tom answered. He looked to the pile of rubble that was once a family home and let out a long breath. "Eesh, hell of a case to come back from medical leave on."

"We'll help however we can, sir," Velez said. Yeah, she definitely reminded Simone of herself as a young firefighter—right down to the suck-up tendencies.

"And now that you've got all the labor you need, I should probably get back to the office and find out what fresh hell is waiting for me there," Amelia said. "I'll leave Kelsey to finish the forensics on the scene."

The mention of the ME's office reminded Simone that this wasn't the only destroyed neighborhood this morning. She looked at the refrigerated truck and wondered how many more there were stationed around Fox City. The thought turned her stomach.

"Good luck," she said to Amelia, who gave her a wan smile.

"Thanks."

She watched Amelia remove her exam gloves and pack up her investigation kit. Simone couldn't bring herself to ask for Amelia's phone number in the middle of a mass disaster, with so many dead around the city. It seemed callous, so Simone just had to hope their paths would cross again—in a more cheerful setting, preferably.

Amelia walked to the refrigerated truck and had a brief conversation with the driver through his window. He got out and together they stowed the ramps and secured the roll door, then Amelia climbed into the passenger side. The truck drove slowly out of the neighborhood, and Simone turned back to her recruits.

Kelsey was giving them instructions for processing

the scene, and Simone used her radio to call over any other available members of her crew. They started at the perimeter. There were two exterior walls still standing, giving the structure the look of a life-sized doll house with two sides cut away.

The kitchen on the ground floor was still mostly intact, as were the stairs to the basement where both victims and survivors had been found. There was also a lot of rubble and splintered shards of wood down there, fallen from the crumbled upper levels. Through all that, Simone could see the broken pool table two of the victims had attempted to shelter under.

She stayed on the lawn while Tom, Kelsey and the probies carefully explored inside. Her job was watching them all, listening for any indication that the structure was imminently unstable, and she didn't breathe for the first few minutes. It all held, though, and the probies cleared the staircase so Tom and Kelsey could get to the basement.

"Oh, wow, look at that!" Larson said. Simone was still turning her head in his direction when she heard the distinctive crack of wood giving way.

"Stop!" she and Tom both shouted.

Larson turned around. "Huh?"

He was on the first floor, standing in what used to be the living room and which now had a sharp drop-off to the basement. He stood slack-jawed as the floorboards snapped beneath his feet, and Simone sprinted to him. She grabbed his hand and yanked him out of the house just as the living room floor dropped six feet into the basement.

Kelsey was down there, fortunately in the opposite corner, and she made a mad dash for the stairs.

"You okay?" Tom called.

She had her back pressed up against the cinderblock wall, panting for breath, but she managed a thumbs up.

"Oh shit," Larson said when the dust settled, looking at the spot where he'd been standing.

"Yeah, oh shit," Simone scowled. "What the hell were you thinking?"

"I'm sorry," Larson said. "I got distracted."

"You can't afford to get distracted," Simone told him. "Not in this job—that's how people get killed."

He nodded. She could have kept yelling at him and the other recruits just to make sure they also learned his lesson, but he looked as if he might cry. She relented—this was a hard day for everyone, and she couldn't imagine how she would have felt if her first day as a firefighter had been like this.

Truth be told, she was a little surprised none of her recruits had quit on her.

"You're all doing a good job," she said. "But you can't let your guard down."

Larson nodded, and Williams and Velez looked sufficiently warned too.

"So," she asked, "what the hell distracted you?"

"There's a gun safe in the rubble down there," he said. "The kind people use for rifles."

"You sure?" Tom asked.

Larson nodded. "My dad has one just like it."

"Well, we're going to have to get it out of there," Tom said. "If we're real lucky, we'll find the gun used on Jane Doe and that'll answer some big questions."

"Those things are heavy," Larson said. "A couple hundred pounds at the least."

"And I can't let anyone go back in there after the floor collapsed," Simone said. "It's not safe."

Tom nodded, thinking for a moment. "I'll make some calls, see about bringing in a crane to lift it out."

"Sweet, like a giant claw game?" Williams asked. Simone scowled at him and he clapped his mouth shut.

7

AMELIA

*T*he next day, the skies were still overcast and it drizzled on and off all morning, but the threat of more storms appeared to have passed. Amelia heard from Reese that the previous day's tornado had been an F4, classified as causing 'devastating damage.'

It had certainly been devastating for the families of all the victims in the three refrigerated trucks now parked outside her office, awaiting identification and autopsy. There were three dozen in all, the worst mass fatality Amelia had ever personally seen and the worst tragedy Fox City had endured in a single day.

Of course, the opiate epidemic still raged, and took the lives of more than three dozen people every year in this city. But to see death on this scale, all those bodies tucked into black plastic bags and stored en masse... it was crushing.

Amelia went about her work feeling as if somebody

had turned the gravity up on the world, pulling her shoulders down and making each step feel heavy.

"Hey, you doing okay?" Jordan asked in the afternoon when they were finishing up yet another autopsy.

She was Amelia's assistant, and most of the time she was boisterous and jovial to the point that Amelia sometimes needed to remind her to be professional. It was her coping mechanism to get through a job that was otherwise morbid, but today, even Jordan didn't have any jokes or pranks in her arsenal.

"Yeah, just tired," Amelia said.

She'd barely taken a break since yesterday. There was too much work to do, a city to rebuild. She was hungry, her feet hurt, she had to pee like mad, and a bubble bath with a glass of chilled white wine would be absolutely heavenly. That last wish list item would have to wait until those three refrigerated trucks were emptied out and sent back where they'd come from.

Nobody else was taking a break, and as the chief, Amelia sure as hell couldn't. All five of the autopsy tables were in use, something Amelia had rarely seen. The morgue was noisy with the voices of five doctors, five assistants, five attending police officers. And it'd stay that way for the foreseeable future.

There was just one thing Amelia couldn't ignore.

"Nature calls," she said as she finished stitching up the Y-shaped incision she'd made on the body cavity of the present victim. "Let's take a ten-minute break before we move on to the next case."

"Sounds good, Dr. T," Jordan said. "I could use a Red Bull."

Amelia grimaced. "I don't know how you drink that stuff."

"I don't know how you don't," Jordan countered. "Especially on a day like today."

"Coffee is more than enough for me," she said. "I can't afford to get the shakes."

In fact, a hot cup of coffee sounded damn good right about then. She finished her work and helped Jordan move the body onto a gurney, then stripped off her gloves and gown.

First, drain the bladder which had been aching for far too long. Then, coffee.

She headed out of the morgue toward the front of the office. The lab technicians, Dylan and Elise, were just as busy as the pathologists, and the investigators were all furiously typing up scene reports for each of the tornado victims. Amelia used the restroom, then made a beeline for the break room. She'd nearly gotten there when someone called, "Dr. Trace."

She turned to see Tom Logan coming up the hall— with a familiar, very attractive firefighter.

Simone looked different without all the heavy gear she'd been wearing on the scene yesterday. Today she was in her station uniform, a pair of navy slacks and a button-up shirt with a Fox County Fire Department patch on her arm.

"Simone," Amelia said, sounding breathless—because

she'd been rushing or because Simone stole her breath away, she honestly didn't know. "Hi."

"How are you doing with all this?" she asked.

"Getting through it." Suddenly Amelia's feet didn't hurt quite as bad and she didn't feel her hunger as much. The bubble bath would still be nice though. Especially if she wasn't alone...

She pushed the thought away. Talk about reminding someone of their professionalism!

"What are you doing here?" she asked.

Simone gave her a wry smile. "Don't sound so happy to see me."

"I didn't mean it like that," Amelia said. "It's just been chaotic around here. I figured the fire station would be the same way."

"Oh, it definitely is," Simone said. "But I've got the probies restocking supplies and I figured that would keep them busy long enough to pop over here with Tom for a few minutes."

"Simone and her crew did a lot of work on the scene yesterday after you left," he said. "I figured she'd be interested to see it through."

Amelia studied his face. She knew from what Kelsey had told her that he'd been instrumental in the early stages of her relationship with Officer Zara Hayes by letting Zara shadow a case Kelsey was investigating. And then there was Zara's patrol partner and the police chief's daughter—he'd bent the rules for them too, and now they were happily dating. Was the gruff homicide detective and confirmed bachelor a secret matchmaker?

Not that Amelia needed it. She already knew that Simone was the most gorgeous woman she'd seen in a very long time, *and* she knew that she didn't have room for romance—during the mass disaster or any other time. So while she loved the way Simone made her feel, and she loved looking at her, that was as far as it could go.

Or maybe she was reading way too deeply into all of it. She turned her attention back to the case at hand.

"I wish I had more to report about Jane Doe from my end of things," she said. "Ordinarily I would have done the autopsy by now, or at least scheduled it. We've got three dozen bodies in the refrigerated trucks and the other pathologists and I have just been autopsying them in the order that we pull them out. We're doing our best just to keep the process moving."

"Understandable," Tom said. "I'm not so concerned with the actual autopsy right now, but I was hoping you could take a closer look at that bullet wound today. Simone, tell her what your recruit found."

"There was a gun safe in the basement of the house," she told Amelia.

"I talked to the homeowner, Cal," Tom added. "He told me that his wife knew the combination, and he'd recently told it to his son too, since the boy was getting older. Cal wanted him to have access for personal safety reasons in case Cal himself wasn't home."

"And you want to know if the caliber of the bullet matches one of the guns inside?" Amelia asked. "Come on, let's have some coffee while we talk."

"Exactly," Tom said as she led them to the break

room. "Cal owns a few hunting rifles and a .22 for home defense, says they should all be accounted for in the safe. We haven't actually been able to retrieve it yet, though— I'm on a damn waiting list for a crane."

Amelia poured them each a cup of coffee and offered cream and sugar. Tom loaded his up with plenty of both, and Simone added a dash of cream to hers. Tom told Amelia he wanted to know the bullet caliber for when they did eventually excavate the safe, and his next step would be going to the hospital to talk to the two injured boys now that they were out of the woods.

"One of them needed surgery," he said. "And the Thomas boy, Noah, ended up needing a blood transfusion. Apparently he's a universal recipient, though, so that's lucky, and he's doing well now. Cal said he would probably get released today and I want to get over to the hospital before that happens so I can question them both at once."

"I'm sure the Thomases are in no hurry to leave," Simone said. "It's not like they have a home to go back to at the moment."

Amelia got to the bottom of her coffee cup entirely too quickly, and she figured it was probably past the ten minutes she'd told Jordan she would be gone. "Should we go look at that bullet?"

Tom nodded, and Amelia took their coffee mugs, then led them through the building to the morgue in the back. Tom was here on at least a weekly basis so she knew he'd be fine, and she guessed from Simone's calm demeanor yesterday that she'd be okay too, but it was always nice to get a read on people. She'd had plenty of fainters in the past.

"Have you been back here before?" Amelia asked her.

Simone nodded. "Once, during training, and a couple of times to deliver bodies from fire scenes."

"Well, it's a lot busier than usual right now," Amelia warned her.

"Don't worry, I can handle it."

Amelia nodded. "I'm sure you can."

They went into the morgue, where the other four docs were still hard at work. Jordan was sitting on the counter and she hopped down the minute she saw Amelia. How many times had she told that girl there were more than enough stools and chairs in this office?

Amelia resisted rolling her eyes, and Jordan asked, "Ready for the next one?"

"Not just yet," Amelia said. "Can you come outside and help us locate a body?"

Jordan nodded and pulled on a pair of gloves. Amelia did the same, then passed the box around. The four of them went through the rear door, where three identical tractor trailers were parked, their refrigeration units quietly humming.

Amelia pointed to the middle truck, the one that had been on Balch Street yesterday. Jordan unlocked and rolled up the door, and they all climbed aboard.

"We're looking for Jane Doe number eight," Amelia told them.

"Eight?" Simone repeated. "That's awful."

Amelia nodded. "Don't worry—we'll find out who all these people belong to."

There were small identifying tags attached to the zippers of each body bag. They all hunted around until, a minute later, Tom said, "Here she is."

"Do you need anything more than the caliber of the gun today?" Amelia asked. "We're still working on truck number one right now, but I can bump her autopsy up the list."

"No, you've got a system going," Tom said. "Just the caliber is fine for now."

Amelia unzipped the body bag and felt Simone draw in a breath beside her. Jane Doe had only been dead about twenty-four hours, and the refrigeration had arrested decay for the time being, but she was much paler now than she'd been yesterday. She was tragically young, and laid out like this, it was obvious that her neck had been broken, probably thanks to the high winds.

"Are you sure you're okay?" Amelia asked softly.

Simone nodded. "She's just a kid. And what's wrong with her arms?"

Amelia followed the direction of Simone's gaze. She was looking at the purplish splotches on her triceps. "It's called livor mortis—her blood has settled on the lower portions of her body because her heart's no longer moving it through her veins."

Simone sighed. "When I encounter dead bodies on the job, it's usually right after they passed, or I'm holding them as they die."

"That's a very difficult thing to handle," Amelia said.

It had happened to her a couple of times during medical school, and that helpless feeling was a large part of the reason she'd gone into forensic pathology, where she could avoid it.

She pulled the sides of the bag open with Simone's help and found the small evidence bag she'd tucked in with the body, containing the bullet. She held it out to Tom, who grimaced slightly. "Couldn't you have washed off the blood?"

"You're wearing gloves," Amelia pointed out. He took the bag and she zipped Jane Doe back up. "Come back inside and I'll sign that evidence over to you, then you can do whatever you need with it."

She took them back through the morgue, stripping off her gloves as she went, and decided that this was a task they could do in her office so nobody had to endure the sights, sounds and smells of four simultaneous autopsies while they did the paperwork. She told Jordan to prepare the next body, then brought Tom and Simone to her office at the front of the building.

It was a nice room, the best-furnished office in the place since she was the most senior pathologist. Not that she'd chosen any of it—picked by her retired predecessor —or saw it very often. She only ever came here to check emails and write up case findings. And she'd been in her office even less in the last couple of days. Her lunch bag from yesterday was still sitting on her desk, but she'd had no time to eat it.

While Amelia filled out a chain of custody form, Tom lifted the evidence bag to the light of the window. "Looks like a nine-millimeter, but I'll have my forensics guys verify."

"Does that tell you much?" Simone asked.

He snorted. "Not really. Cal Thomas doesn't have one registered, but it's one of the most common calibers out there, so it doesn't narrow down the field of suspects."

"So, what are you thinking?" she asked. "There's no way that many people could have been completely unaware there was a stranger in their house, right?"

"It seems unlikely," Tom conceded. "I showed Cal one of the photos Kelsey took at the scene. Was kind of wondering if he was having an affair or something. He said he'd never seen her before and seemed convincing." He shrugged. "Who knows? One of the teens could be lying about knowing her."

"Why would they?" Simone asked.

"No clue," Tom said. "Who can understand the mind of a teenaged boy?" He tucked the evidence bag into his pocket and said, "Well, I better get this to the police forensics lab, then I'm going over to the hospital before they release Noah."

Amelia held the form out and he folded it, then stuck that in his pocket too. He said goodbye, and then it was just Amelia and Simone in the office.

"You didn't drive over with him?" Amelia asked.

"Nope, I've got my own ride." She was smiling at Amelia, drinking her in. "I'm glad I got to see you again."

Warmth crept up Amelia's neck. Was it wrong how much she liked it?

8

SIMONE

*A*melia was studying Simone openly, like she had when they were in that van together yesterday. Her eyes swept over Simone's face, down to her dark blue uniform, and her lips curled into a smile.

"Did you really come all the way down here just to tell me what your crew found at the scene?" she asked. "Tom could have done that."

Simone shrugged. "Do I really need an excuse to get away from that rag-tag crew for a little while?" Amelia laughed, conceding the point, then Simone added, "Plus, I kind of wanted to see the chief ME in her domain."

Amelia looked down at the wrinkled scrubs she was wearing and said, "I'm afraid it's not that impressive at the moment. We're all just trying to keep our heads above water."

"You're not the only ones," Simone answered.

"Speaking of, I should get back," Amelia said. "Jordan's probably ready for the next autopsy."

"When's the last time you ate?" Simone asked. She'd noticed the lunch bag on Amelia's desk when they first sat down. It looked like the type you normally keep refrigerated, and from the way Amelia had been talking, it seemed unlikely that she'd take the time to eat it in any case.

Amelia looked toward the ceiling, trying to recall. "I had a peanut butter sandwich for dinner yesterday."

"Well, it's past lunchtime now," Simone pointed out. She stood and beckoned Amelia with a wave of her hand. "Come on, there's a food truck parked a block away."

Amelia shook her head. "I can't. Jordan's waiting for me and–"

"You can, or you might end up collapsing on the job," Simone said. When Amelia still hesitated, she added, "I'm a firefighter—I know how to take care of people. You need to eat."

She didn't mention that her own stomach was also rumbling, but there was a good chance Amelia had heard it anyway.

"Jordan–"

"–can wait," Simone finished for her. "Especially if you bring her something from the truck."

Amelia rolled her eyes and laughed. "You sure are persistent. One minute." She picked up her desk phone and called back to the morgue to tell Jordan where she was going. She promised to be quick and bring food for everybody working back there. Then she hung up the receiver and stood. "Okay, let's go."

Simone laughed. "Don't act so much like I'm leading

you to the gallows. It's just street food. What do you have in that sad little lunch bag, anyway?"

"A day-old egg salad sandwich," Amelia said, and Simone made a face.

"Eww, and you kept it on your desk?"

Now it was Amelia's turn to laugh, an unrestrained one that lit up her whole face and was quite beautiful. "Not intentionally. I think I dropped it in the parking lot yesterday when the tornado siren was going off. Somebody must have found it afterward and left it here for me."

"Well, let me help you with it," Simone said, dumping the contents into a trash bin beside the desk. "Now, let's get some decent food. I'm glad I insisted."

Amelia nodded, her gray eyes sparkling. "Me too."

Outside, the weather had turned to a fine mist, uncomfortable, like being a vegetable at the grocery store when the sprinklers turned on. Amelia fished an umbrella out of her bag and opened it between them. It was small, so they had to huddle together as they walked, and that was fine by Simone.

"Let me hold that," she offered. "I'm taller."

Amelia appraised her. "Only by a couple of inches."

Simone took the umbrella anyway, fighting the urge to wrap her arm around Amelia's shoulder. She could smell the rich, sweet aroma of her perfume, alluring even though it was underscored by the antiseptic smell of the ME's office.

"I'm glad you decided to take a break with me," she

said as they walked. "I was contemplating forcibly dragging you out if you didn't agree."

Amelia laughed. "Honestly, I wouldn't have minded if you did. I don't know if you noticed, but I tend to be a bit of a workaholic."

Now it was Simone's turn to laugh. She let her eyes go mockingly wide and said, "No way."

Amelia bumped her shoulder. "I'm sure you know what it's like as a woman in a male-dominated field. It's hard to make people take you seriously unless you work twice as hard as everyone else."

"Oh, trust me, I've told way more dick jokes than I ever wanted to, all in the name of being 'one of the guys,'" Simone said. "I want to make captain one day, though, so I do what it takes."

"Will that be a difficult climb?" Amelia asked.

"I hope not," Simone said. "I became a lieutenant relatively young, and the guys all respect me. Proving that I've got leadership skills—particularly while I'm training the probies—will go a long way toward showing them that I'm ready for the promotion. What about you, Ms. Chief Medical Examiner?"

"I sort of got lucky," Amelia said. "Don't get me wrong, I worked my ass off all through medical school and my residency. But I started working for Fox County about five years before the previous chief retired, and we really clicked professionally. He took me under his wing and basically mentored me into the position. I'm trying to pay it forward now with Kelsey—she's going to med school."

They talked easily all the way to the food truck, without any of the awkward silences that were so common in the *getting to know you* stages of a new relationship. Their shoulders were pressed together in an effort to stay under the small umbrella... or maybe that was just an excuse to be close to each other. Simone liked to think it was the latter.

When they got to the food truck, there was no line thanks to the weather. This one was of the Mexican persuasion and Simone barely needed to glance at the menu. She went first since she was only ordering for herself and Amelia was ordering for half her staff, but when she reached for her wallet, Amelia batted her hand away.

"Let me get your lunch."

"I can't let you do that," Simone said. "It'd hurt my pride."

"Consider it a thank you for getting me out of the office for a few minutes," Amelia insisted. She used her hip to playfully shove Simone aside, then added her own order and two dozen assorted tacos for her staff.

She paid and they went over to a picnic table to wait.

"You better sit beside me—otherwise I don't think the umbrella can cover us both," Simone said.

They sat with their backs to the table, looking out at the street. From here, Simone could see a little way down the road toward downtown, and it looked completely unremarkable. Sitting here, you'd never know there were three dozen dead from a tornado that had ravaged the city only the day before.

It just looked like an ordinary rainy day.

Ordinary except for the gorgeous woman whose hip was pressed up against Simone's on the picnic bench beside her.

While they waited for their food, Simone quizzed Amelia about herself—what got her into forensic pathology, what she did outside of work... and whether there was a significant other in the picture. It never hurt to ask.

At that, Amelia laughed. "You heard the part about me working twice as hard as everyone else, right? What makes you think I have time to date?"

Simone smiled. "I get the impression you don't take much time for yourself in general. But I can't talk—I'm always either at the firehouse or on call, especially now that I'm trying to move up the ladder."

"Not down the fireman's pole, so to speak?"

"Poles have never been my thing," Simone said, and Amelia snorted.

"Me neither."

"Would you want a partner if you did have time?"

"Yeah, of course," Amelia said. She didn't even hesitate and that made Simone smile. "You?"

"Yeah."

"Do you ever worry about it?" Amelia asked.

"About what?"

"We're already working our asses off as women in male-dominated fields," she said. "Add a girlfriend into the mix–"

It was something Simone had thought about—of course she had. But she shook her head, adamant. "I decided a long time ago that I wasn't going to let anyone tell me that my sexual orientation affects my performance as a firefighter. And I've been fortunate—everyone I've worked with has been accepting." She smirked and added, "Only I'm allowed to let my career keep me from finding love."

Amelia laughed. "Sounds like you should stop standing in your own way."

"What about you?" Simone asked.

Amelia smiled. It started as just a small curl of the lips, then turned into a full-on grin. "You'd be surprised how many queer women there are working in the medical examiner's office. It's not a problem at all, so we're all lucky too."

"And yet you're not dating any of them?" Simone asked.

Amelia looked at her like she was crazy. "They're all my subordinates. It would be wildly unethical."

"Lucky for me," Simone answered. "I don't work for you."

Then the taco truck owner leaned out the window with a couple big bags stuffed with food. "Order up!"

"Do you want to eat here or go back to my office?" Amelia asked.

It was nice being alone out here with her, but Simone pointed to some pretty ominous-looking storm clouds gathering overhead. "Probably safest to go back to your office. Plus I'm feeling pretty damp right about now, like those people who ride the boat right up to the base of Niagara Falls."

"The Maid of the Mist."

"Yeah, that's it."

Simone handed off the umbrella and went to get the food bags. She offered Amelia her elbow, and was surprised when she took it. They ambled back toward the ME's office, and Simone told Amelia about the time she and a bunch of high school friends went up to Ontario to hang out in the casinos for a weekend for no other reason than that they were old enough to gamble in Canada.

"I ended up getting drunk and kissing my best friend, who was *not* into it," she said, cringing at the memory. "Not my finest weekend."

Amelia wrinkled her nose in sympathy. "Did it ruin the friendship?"

"For a while," Simone said. "But we got over the awkwardness and I learned how to read signals better. Which is not to say that was my last crush on a straight girl."

Amelia laughed. "Story of my college life. Small, conservative campus, slim pickings for baby gay Amelia."

"I bet she was adorable though," Simone said. "I woulda gone for it."

She laughed again. "How old are you, anyway? Were you in elementary school when I was in college?"

Simone feigned offense. "I'm not that much younger than you."

"Are you sure?" Amelia challenged. "How old do you think I am?"

Oh shit... she'd walked right into that trap and she may have been younger than Amelia, but she was old enough to know that was one question you never wanted to have to answer—especially when you were crushing hard on the asker. She thought for a second, then said, "Old enough to have crazy-attractive confidence, and young enough to take a chance on my dumb ass. I hope."

Amelia snorted. "Good save."

"Thank you." Simone breathed a sigh of relief.

"I'm forty-two," she said, studying Simone for a reaction.

"Middle school."

"Huh?"

"I would have been eleven when you were starting college," Simone answered. "That's not even close to an appropriate relationship, but I'm thirty-three now."

They were turning into the parking lot of the ME's office, and Amelia pointed toward the refrigerated trucks.

"Let's go in the back door," she said. "I didn't buy enough food for everybody so it wouldn't be fair to trail the scent of tacos through the halls."

"Playing favorites?" Simone teased.

"More like being realistic about how many tacos it was fair to ask that poor guy at the food truck to make," Amelia said. "I should definitely buy the whole staff pizza or something this week, though."

"Good idea. Maybe I could bring my crew over and they can all mingle," Simone suggested. It was purely an excuse to spend more time with Amelia, but she managed to bullshit her way into a pretty good idea. "Firefighters and death investigators don't see each other all that much in the field, but our paths do cross. It'd probably be good to get to know each other better."

Amelia nodded. "I like that idea."

Just then, the sky dimmed. In the space of a second, it was twilight, and Amelia looked up at the dark clouds above them. Simone dragged Amelia over to the narrow overhang above the back door just as the sky opened up and it began to pour.

"Why does this keep happening to us?" Amelia laughed, quickly rolling up the bottoms of her scrubs to keep them from getting soaked.

"Bad omen?" Simone suggested, though she hoped it wasn't that.

"Maybe the opposite—the universe wants us to get closer," Amelia said, the reply surprising Simone. She collapsed the umbrella—it wasn't doing them much good under the awning—and took the takeout bags out of Simone's hands, putting them on a bench next to the door.

And then she brought both hands up to Simone's cheeks, cupping her head in her hands and stepping closer. Their lips touched, and Simone breathed Amelia in, that heady, warm scent that made her dizzy in the best possible way. She tasted sweet, and it felt so right to hold her close in the rain.

It was something she'd been daydreaming about since it had almost happened yesterday. It was well worth the wait.

When she pulled back, Simone said, "I think I'm pretty good at signal reading now."

"If you were, you wouldn't have stopped kissing me," Amelia answered.

And so, never one to need telling twice, Simone kissed her again—deeper, longer, drinking in everything about the moment and loving it.

9

DERIKA

*D*erika Moore was bleeding from a head wound beneath her hairline. The blood flowed down her forehead and over one eye, and when she caught sight of herself in a shop window, she looked like a victim from a slasher flick.

Felt like one too.

Had he hit her, or did she get cut by some debris while she was staggering through the high winds away from him? She couldn't remember, and she supposed it didn't really matter. All that mattered was that she'd gotten away.

Escaped. With her life.

Head wounds bleed more than cuts on other parts of your body. She remembered learning that somewhere— from her father, maybe? He shaved his head a lot when she was a kid. Clearly it was true because it had been quite a while since she escaped and the blood was still flowing. Did she need stitches? Was all this going to end in a hospital, or a police station, giving her statement and hoping the cops took her seriously?

If she could just go home and never think about all this again, she'd be happy. But in her gut, she knew that wasn't an option. If she didn't tell someone, he'd just do it again to some other unsuspecting girl.

When she turned a corner, brushing her shoulder against the brick building and feeling a little woozy, she realized she was downtown. Back where all this had started. She knew where she was again at last—the only thing she didn't know was how long she'd been lost and wandering.

She kept going, steeling herself to find help, tell her story. She walked two more blocks in the direction of the Fox County Police Department, and then stopped when she stepped in front of an open garage bay and saw a massive, bright red fire engine. Relief washed over her. Firefighters were trained in first aid, weren't they? Firefighters took in abandoned babies and handled all sorts of other situations where people were reluctant—or afraid—to go to the police.

And they didn't carry guns.

They didn't kneel on innocent, unsuspecting Black civilians until they couldn't breathe.

The firefighters, they were safe. Or at least relatively so.

Derika stepped inside the building, and she didn't even have to announce herself. Before she could open her mouth, a tall, athletically built woman in a navy uniform rushed over to her.

Derika must have looked even worse than she thought because the woman's face betrayed horror at what she saw.

"Oh my God, what happened to you?" she asked, putting her hand on Derika's elbow. She was supporting her as if she were about to fall down, and it wasn't until she felt the woman's arm wrapping securely around her back that she realized how exhausted she was.

Her legs momentarily gave out on her and Derika slumped toward the concrete floor. The woman held her up long enough for the swoon to end and for Derika to stand under her own power again. Then she guided her over to a table off to one side of the garage.

"Sit," she said, her hands going to Derika's head the moment she'd landed in the chair. "Are you wounded anywhere other than your scalp?"

Derika shook her head, although she wasn't totally sure that was true. She didn't remember getting hurt anywhere else, but she didn't remember how she'd gotten the head wound either. "I don't think so."

"Stay right here," the woman ordered, and she said it with such authority that Derika didn't even consider the alternative. "I'm going to get a first aid kit. I'll be right back."

Derika nodded, her eyelids suddenly feeling so heavy. It was as if the moment she'd gotten off her feet, every ounce of the exhaustion that she hadn't allowed herself to feel in the last twenty-four hours hit her all at once. Like her body knew that she was in a safe space now and it was okay to be vulnerable again.

She was holding back tears when the woman returned. She set down a large first aid kit on the table, along with a folded blanket, then pulled a chair up next to Derika's. "I brought you a blanket. You must be freezing."

It wasn't until she'd said it that Derika realized she *was* cold. And her clothes were drenched. It had been raining off and on all day. She gladly accepted the blanket, wrapping it around her shoulders.

"Is it okay if I sit next to you and clean you up a bit?" the woman asked.

Derika nodded, swallowing back those tears. Her throat felt thick with them, but now they stemmed from gratitude instead of fear and exhaustion. "Thank you."

"My name is Simone," the woman said. "I'm a lieutenant here." She reached for a bottle of saline and some gauze. "What's your name?"

Her voice was soft and comforting, and Derika tilted her head to make it easier for her to take care of the cut.

"I'm Derika," she said. "Moore."

Cool liquid trickled down her scalp and into the gauze that Simone held against her temple. Saline, or blood? Derika wondered if she was overdue for a tetanus shot.

"Is it bad?" she asked.

Simone shook her head. "It's deep, but only about an inch long. I feel confident that you'll live."

Derika smiled. How was she smiling right now, when minutes ago she'd been on the verge of tears, terrified and confused?

Well, she was still confused. But it was nice to feel calm.

"Derika, did someone do this to you?" Simone asked, cautious like she'd had to ask the question too many times before. She probably thought Derika had an abusive husband or boyfriend, that she was a battered woman. Well, she had been battered, but not by anyone she knew.

"Yes," she said softly. "But there was so much going on... the winds..."

"Tornado," Simone said, and Derika arched her brows.

"Really?"

"You didn't know?" Simone asked. "It touched down in three different places around the city."

"Are people dead?" Derika asked. Suddenly those tears were welling up again. What she was doing here, taking up the lieutenant's time, when there were other people who had it so much worse?

"Let's just focus on you right now, okay?" Simone said. It was like she could read Derika's mind, saw the guilt festering there. She must have been at this job for a long time because she was damn good at it. She reached for a little bottle of liquid bandage and said, "I'm going to try this and we'll see if it holds. If not, you'll need stitches."

Derika nodded, then sat still while Simone worked. It didn't take her long to apply the adhesive, then she laid a gauze pad over the wound and wrapped an elastic bandage around her head to hold it in place. Then she offered her bottled water or coffee.

"Coffee would be amazing," Derika said, positively salivating for a warm beverage. "I feel like I could fall asleep sitting right here."

"Well, don't do that—you could have a concussion," Simone said. She disappeared for another minute or two and came back with two steaming mugs of coffee on a tray, plus cream and sugar.

"I wasn't sure how you take it."

Derika poured equal amounts of both into her mug.

While she stirred, Simone asked, "Will you tell me what happened to you, Derika?"

She smiled again, this one more of a grimace. "I barely remember."

"You said it happened during the tornado," Simone observed. "That was yesterday. Where have you been since then?"

Derika furrowed her brow. "I was looking for help, I think. This is the first place I stopped."

"In a full day?" Simone questioned. When Derika gave her a blank, helpless look, she explained, "The tornado hit Monday morning. It's Tuesday afternoon now."

"Oh." She was missing an entire day of her life. Had she passed out? Was she wandering around in a fugue state that entire time? It would explain why she was so damn tired. "Wow."

Simone put her hand on Derika's forearm. "What *do* you remember, hon?"

Derika took a deep breath. She tried to remember even though parts of her brain didn't want her to. Right before she came to the firehouse, she'd been thinking that it was important to tell someone what he did to her... it looked like she'd found that someone.

She dug deep, sorting out all the fuzzy, confusing thoughts and memories. "I was going to work. I've been taking rideshares since last week because my car broke down. He was weird from the start."

"Your driver?"

She nodded, thinking about him. She got lost in that thought, and Simone had to prompt her to continue.

"Weird how?"

"Friendly, but like, excessively," Derika said. "Like we were speed dating instead of him driving me to work and then never seeing me again. And then when we got downtown, he drove right past my office. That was when I noticed there were no handles on the insides of the passenger doors."

"He tried to abduct you?" Simone asked.

"He *did* abduct me," Derika said, all of it becoming clearer the more she talked. The panic, the complete and utter helplessness of being locked in the back of his car. "I don't know where he was taking me—somewhere downtown, not too far from my office. He pulled over and he was about to drag me out of the car when the siren went off."

"The tornado siren?"

"Must have been," Derika nodded. "He looked up to see what was happening and I kicked him as hard as I possibly could and got the hell out of there."

"Good for you," Simone said.

"I hope I ruptured his testicle," Derika said, her body tensing at the thought of him. When he'd reached into the back seat, ready to haul her out and do God-knows-what to her, she'd felt physical sickness and a visceral terror more real than anything she'd ever felt before. Just thinking of him now made those feelings rise up her gullet again.

"I do too," Simone said with a smirk. "So you got away in the middle of the tornado? That's incredible."

"I was running on pure adrenaline," Derika admitted. "I can't remember what happened after that."

"You got away," Simone said. "That's what matters. I know that's a lot to go through, but do you feel up to giving an official statement about what happened? I can call a police officer to come over here—you won't even have to leave the firehouse."

Derika nodded. "I can do that."

"Good," Simone said. "We can't let this guy strike again, and he needs to pay for what he did to you."

"With more than just his testicle," Derika said, and this time they both did more than just smile. They actually laughed, and it felt good.

10

AMELIA

*I*t wasn't until the end of the week that Amelia finally got to autopsy Jane Doe number eight. She'd asked the other pathologists to leave it for her, and they were all making steady but slow progress through the tornado victims.

By Friday afternoon, they were down to two refrigerated trucks in the parking lot, having released about a dozen victims to their families and various funeral homes around the city. So far they were all deaths by natural causes, but there was obviously more to Jane Doe number eight's story.

Amelia had Jordan prepare the body for autopsy right after lunch, and she'd arranged for Tom to come observe, as was protocol in any kind of criminal death investigation. She was putting on her paper gown and exam gloves when he came into the morgue, and she was a little disappointed to see that he was alone this time.

"No Lieutenant Olivier?" she asked, trying to sound casual.

"No reason for her to be here," Tom pointed out. He narrowed his eyes, studying her. "What, do you have a crush on her or something?"

"No!" Amelia said a little too quickly.

"What am I, the official wingman of the Fox County lesbian community?" Tom asked. "This is three times now, you know."

"I have no clue what you're talking about," Amelia said. She couldn't help cracking a smile as she added, "You *are* good at it, though."

"Apparently," he said, approaching the autopsy table with a faint limp.

"Still hurting?" she asked, nodding to the thigh that had taken a bullet.

"Had an occupational therapy session at lunch," Tom explained. "Always hurts like a bitch afterward."

Amelia arched an eyebrow. "Hurts like a what?"

Tom looked sufficiently ashamed as he said, "Hurts like crazy."

Amelia smirked, then turned her attention to Jordan, who was coming over with Jane Doe's X-rays.

"Hot off the printer," she said, then clipped them to a view box near the autopsy table.

Amelia and Tom both went over to look. As a seasoned homicide detective, Tom had been around the block a few times and he was perfectly capable of identifying major fractures, but that didn't make him a radiographer. Amelia pointed to the cervical spine and talked him through what she was seeing.

"Basal skull fracture," she said, using her gloved hand to point to the base of the skull, then to the spine just below it, "with grade three dislocation of the C_1 vertebra."

"And in layman's terms?" Tom asked.

"The back of her head was hit hard enough to fracture her skull and torque her vertebrae out of alignment," Amelia said. "We see this type of injury most commonly in falls down a flight of stairs."

"Well, that fits what we know so far," Tom agreed. "I got details from Simone since I wasn't there when she pulled the body out of the house. She said Jane Doe was found near the base of the stairs, not at the other end of the basement where we found the others."

"So it's possible they really didn't know she was in the house. With all the chaos, it's plausible that they wouldn't have heard or seen someone falling down the stairs," Amelia said.

"What about the gunshot?" Tom asked.

Amelia frowned. "Jordan, will you help me turn her?"

They rotated the body on the stainless-steel table, face-down.

The girl's hair was what some call dirty blonde, made dirtier by all that she'd gone through. Amelia parted her hair carefully, looking for a wound.

"If she hit the back of her head, she must have either

fallen or been pushed backward from the top of the stairs," Tom surmised.

"Likely," Amelia said. She almost never gave a definite answer, especially at this stage in an examination. In her line of work, assumptions were dangerous. They led to missed details and sloppy work. "She died in the middle of a tornado, so we really can't account for what the high winds could have done in regard to the orientation of her body. Here, look."

She took Jane Doe's head carefully in both hands, tilting her chin toward her chest to expose a long, straight gash at the base of her skull, right across the occipital bone. There was matted blood there, previously covered by her long hair.

"I'll examine this wound closer once I'm finished with the rest of the external examination, but a cut like this is consistent with hitting the edge of a stair tread, especially the square-edged type commonly found in basements."

She moved on, noting a few more cuts and scrapes most likely associated with the fall, then asked Jordan to help her roll the victim onto her back again. There were far fewer injuries to the front of the body, consistent with a backward fall. Then she got to the gunshot wound on the upper left arm.

"Did you find out the caliber of the bullet?" she asked Tom.

He nodded. "Nine-mil, like I thought. None of the Thomases have one registered, and I finally got that crane to extract the gun safe. Just like Cal said, there were a couple hunting rifles and a .22, all accounted for. So we're still on the hunt for a nine-millimeter."

"Maybe one of the kids brought it," Jordan interjected. Amelia had briefed her on the case earlier in the week, and while she ordinarily would have reminded Jordan that speculating wasn't part of her job, Tom seemed interested. "I had a friend in high school who used to flash his dad's gun, trying to impress us or make us think he was a bad ass."

"I'll see if any of the parents have nine-mils registered," Tom said.

Amelia shook her head. "I don't think the kids could have shot her. At least not from the basement."

"Why do you say that?" Tom asked.

"She was shot in the left bicep," she pointed out. "If she fell backward down the stairs, that arm would have been next to the cinderblock wall. Besides, the angle's all wrong. She was shot in the front of the arm on a downward trajectory. Whoever shot her was standing in front of her."

"What if she got all the way into the basement and one of the kids thought she was an intruder, shot her in self-defense? Then she fled and was on the stairs when the tornado hit," Tom posited. "I wouldn't at all be surprised if a kid lied about that—hell, some adults don't have the sense to come clean in a situation like that."

Amelia shook her head again, though. "If she was running up the stairs, she most likely would have fallen forward, not backward. We'd see at least *some* injury to the front of her body."

"Okay, so she was shot before she reached the stairs, or on them," Tom said. "By someone who was either standing above her or taller than her."

"That's what the physical evidence is telling me," Amelia answered. "How tall is the husband again?"

"Six-two," Tom said. "Would that put him at the right height to cause this injury?"

"Well, I'm not Dexter, but it's possible," Amelia said. "Are you sure he doesn't know our Jane Doe?"

"I'll have to talk to him again," Tom said. He let out a frustrated breath. "If he doesn't, identifying her is going to be one hell of a job. I'll need a copy of her dental X-rays."

Amelia nodded. "I haven't noticed any distinguishing marks—tattoos, birth marks, scars—but maybe we'll get lucky on the internal examination and find a surgical implant."

She knew the likelihood was slim. The girl was young, not more than twenty by the looks of it, and Amelia hadn't noticed any incision scars. But Tom was looking pretty dejected and she didn't want to squash his hopes.

The rest of the autopsy was fairly unremarkable. Jane Doe appeared to be in good health, with no implants or other identifiers to be found.

"Is it possible that the impact from the gunshot could have caused her to fall backward, if she were shot at the top of the stairs?" Tom asked.

"I doubt it. Because she was shot on the left side of her body, we likely would have seen some twisting, causing her to fall sideways or even front-first," Amelia said. "A backwards fall is more consistent with the effects of the high winds, or a shove."

When she got to the girl's head, which she always left until the end of an autopsy, Tom grimaced. "No matter how many of these I see, I don't think I'll ever get used to watching you peel that skin flap down over the face. That's the only part that bugs me."

Amelia had already cut into the skull, careful to preserve the area that had been fractured. She removed the skull cap in order to examine the brain, explaining, "It's the easiest way to gain entry without compromising the face. Her family can still have an open-casket viewing if they desire, once you find them."

"Yeah, I get it..." he said, purposely avoiding looking at Jane Doe's partially obscured face. "Still creeps me out."

"I think it's kinda cool," Jordan chimed in. "You can pretend she's a cyborg in need of a tune-up if that helps."

Tom gave her a bewildered look. Amelia continued her exam without commenting on Jordan's contribution.

She observed, "There's evidence of traumatic brain injury on the occipital lobe, consistent with a backward fall." She examined the fractured bone and pointed out a faint beveling at the point of impact. "As I suspected, this looks like the type of injury sustained when a person's head comes in contact with a stair tread."

"Is it the cause of death?" Tom asked.

"I'll need to see the toxicology and histology reports,"

Amelia said. "But barring any surprises, yes, I would say so."

"And the manner?" Tom pressed. He was asking Amelia to tell him if this was accidental, a fall down the stairs due to the high winds of the tornado, or if someone did this to Jane Doe.

"I can't make a ruling at this time," Amelia said.

Sometimes cases were open and shut and detectives walked out happy to have one more thing checked off their never-ending to-do lists. More often than not, they got an answer like this one. From the evidence, all Amelia could say was that Jane Doe number eight died as a result of falling down the stairs. She couldn't say whether it was accidental or a homicide, or how the gunshot fit into the narrative.

Figuring that out was Tom's job.

11

NOAH

*N*oah Thomas had been discharged from the hospital about thirty-six hours after he arrived. His friend, Braden, wasn't so lucky. At the beginning of the second week, he was still there, recovering from surgery after his head injury had turned into life-threatening swelling in his brain.

Noah counted himself lucky, especially with two of his friends—and that girl—dead. But after a few days at his aunt's crowded little house, being relentlessly fussed over by his mom, he was all too eager to get out of there. So when David, one of the other survivors, called to suggest they go visit Braden, Noah jumped at the opportunity.

"He's gotta be going out of his mind in that hospital bed," David said.

Noah agreed. "I'm going out of my mind in this house."

"Sounds like a no-brainer, then. Need a lift?"

"Yeah," Noah said. "My Cruze got crunched, and I can't drive with this bum leg anyway."

He'd received twenty stitches in his right calf, and was still changing the bandage a couple times a day. It hurt, but not as much as knowing that some of his closest friends were dead, his house was gone, and on top of all that, the car he'd just gotten for his sixteenth birthday was totaled.

He hadn't actually seen it, but his dad had been by the house with an insurance assessor the previous week and brought back the news that neither Noah's nor his mom's car had survived the tornado. Noah felt guilty every time he found himself mourning the loss of his wheels.

"I'll pick you up in five," David said.

"Thanks, man."

No sooner had Noah ended the call than his mother whipped around the corner from the kitchen, asking, "Are you going somewhere?"

This was what Noah hated about staying at his aunt's place. It was tiny as hell and the walls were paper-thin. Everybody knew everyone else's business, and his mom hadn't stopped hovering around him since they got home from the hospital. He knew she was just worried about him, but that didn't make it any less annoying.

"Yeah, to the hospital," Noah said. "David wants to visit Braden."

"Well, that's sweet," his mom answered. "Let me get my purse, I'll borrow your Aunt Trudy's car."

"*No,*" he said, probably a little too harshly. God, he needed some air, and a little distance.

She shrank back, looking hurt. "How are you going to get there?"

"David's picking me up," he said. Then, because he felt bad for being a dick, he added, "I'll be fine, Mom."

She nodded like she didn't entirely believe him. She'd been acting like he was made of glass ever since they got out of the hospital. He wasn't sure if it was because he'd had to receive a pint of blood and twenty stitches, or because two of his friends were dead. Or because their house was a pile of rubble, and all their earthly possessions were destroyed. Or because there had been a mysterious dead girl in their house and a homicide detective kept calling and coming around to ask questions.

Fuck, there were a lot of things to be upset about these days. And that wasn't even taking into account the fact that his mom had always been a bit of a helicopter parent.

"Are *you* okay, Mom?" he asked. He was pretty much the worst son ever because it had taken him this long to ask her.

Just then, a car horn blared outside—David had made good time.

"I'm okay," Noah's mom said, giving him a smile that wasn't quite convincing. "Go, have fun with your friends."

He rolled his eyes. "We're going to the hospital, not having fun."

"Right. Well, tell Braden I hope he's doing better. Will you be back for dinner?"

Noah glanced at the clock on his phone. It was only two in the afternoon. He was going to get a summer job this year to pay for the gas and insurance on the Cruze. He should have been filling out applications by now, or maybe even flipping burgers or something. All that was uncertain now, and he didn't exactly need the money anymore. It would be nice to have an excuse to regularly leave his aunt's house, though, as soon as his leg healed.

"I'm not sure," he said. "I'll text you."

He hefted himself off the sofa, using a walking stick that used to belong to his grandfather before he passed. Sixteen years old and yet every time he sat down, the part of his calf where the stitches were stiffened up and he *felt* like his grandpa.

"Okay, just keep me in the loop," his mom said. She opened her arms for a hug and Noah figured it was the least he could do to let her have it.

Then he said goodbye and hobbled outside to David's hand-me-down Monte Carlo.

"Could you drive anything lower to the ground?" he asked as he sank awkwardly into the passenger seat.

"What are you, eighty?" David asked. Then he revved the engine, turned up the radio, and they took off down the quiet street. For just a minute, they were a couple of normal teenagers again, careless and free for the summer.

Wouldn't that be nice.

12

AMELIA

*I*t was Tuesday evening, more than a week since the tornado touched down, and Amelia still felt like she was drowning in case files, investigations and mass disaster protocols.

They'd been able to release another dozen bodies to various funeral homes around the county and were now down to just one refrigerated truck in the parking lot. Jane Doe number eight was among the bodies still here, still waiting for identification—a real name, a family who must be missing her. But Amelia had so much paperwork she'd barely been able to think of Jane Doe since the autopsy.

Right now, she was working her way through a big stack of toxicology and histology reports from her lab scientists, Dylan and Elise. The whole staff had been working their asses off and Amelia was proud and grateful.

She'd been serious about that pizza party idea when

she'd pitched it to Simone last week, and deep down she had to admit that it didn't hurt that the party would be an excuse to see the sexy firefighter again. She just had to wait until they'd all gotten sufficiently caught up that they could afford to take a break.

Midway through her paperwork, there was a knock on her doorframe. Because she'd just been thinking of Simone, for a split second Amelia hoped to see her standing there.

Instead, it was Reese. "Bad time?"

Amelia shook her head. "Not at all, come in."

She set aside the toxicology report she'd been looking at—or more like staring glassy-eyed at. She'd been here since seven that morning and she could hear everyone else in the office who worked the day shift preparing to go home. Amelia didn't feel like she could do the same—every time she worked on processing the bodies, paperwork piled up. And the time she spent doing paperwork meant that families had to wait longer for their deceased loved ones to be released.

Besides, other than that fancy new coffee maker, Amelia didn't have a whole lot to go home to. She might as well stay and work.

"What can I do for you?" she asked Reese.

"I just wanted to see how you're doing." Reese was in her early twenties and usually seemed more interested in office gossip than anything else. She caught Amelia off guard tonight.

"Really? That's nice of you."

"I feel bad," Reese explained, still lingering in the

door with one shoulder against the molding. "Everybody else is working so hard, and all I can do is keep answering the phones. I wish I could be more helpful."

"You're plenty helpful," Amelia assured her. "Handling inquiries from family members and the media is very important at a time like this."

Amelia had to hand it to Reese. Despite all the gossiping she did, her work never suffered for it. Same with Jordan, the queen of pranks. When the time came to buckle down, they both did what Amelia needed them to.

"Well, I'm headed home," Reese said. "I mostly came back here to give you this."

She moved away from the doorframe, and Amelia noticed she had a to-go coffee cup in one hand and a takeout bag looped over her wrist. Amelia sat up a little taller, surprised.

"Did you buy me food? I didn't order anything."

In fact, she'd been intending to—ever since lunch. She just hadn't gotten around to it, and without even knowing what was in the bag, her mouth began to water. She'd had no idea how hungry she was until food had suddenly become a real possibility.

"It's not from me," Reese said. "A delivery driver just dropped it off." She set the coffee and the bag on Amelia's desk, then gave her a coy look as she added, "It came with a note."

She pointed to a folded piece of paper taped to the outside of the bag, and Amelia asked, "Did you read it?"

"No," Reese said, not very convincingly. Amelia gave

her a firm look and she raised three fingers in the air. "Scout's honor."

"You're not a Scout," Amelia pointed out. The Scouts hadn't started accepting girls until a few years ago, and by then Reese would have been too old.

"Then I guess you'll just have to take my word," Reese said. "Night, Dr. Trace. Don't stay too late."

She turned on her heel and headed toward the timeclock.

"Good night," Amelia called, distracted by the takeout bag on her desk. She would be willing to bet that Reese had peeked at the note—it was her nature—but at least she'd pretended not to be a snoop.

Amelia flipped the paper open.

I have a feeling you've been skipping meals again... that and Tom told me your case load is still insane. Hope you like burgers and fries—this is from my favorite place near the fire house. I ordered you a coffee too, in case you're working late.

Oh, and give me a call sometime... we need to plan that inter-office pizza lunch.

Simone

She'd included her phone number next to a hand-drawn winky face, and Amelia had to sit back in her chair for a minute as a grin spread over her lips. This was the most thoughtful thing anybody had done for her in a long time—maybe ever—and it had turned her whole evening around.

She took a sip of the coffee, not surprised to find that Simone had remembered how she liked it. Then she picked her phone up and tapped in Simone's number. A call the minute she'd gotten the note might be a little too forward, too eager, but a text...

Got the food you sent, you have no idea how hungry I was. When do you want to collect your gratuity?

It was flirtier than she was used to being, especially with someone who worked for the county and was technically a coworker. But she couldn't help it. As much as she tried not to, as much as she knew there was no room in her life for romance, Simone was irresistible.

Amelia set aside all her paperwork for a few minutes, opening the takeout container and spreading a few napkins out on her desk. The burger was big and juicy, and as she sank her teeth into it, her thoughts lingered on Simone.

Her shaggy brown hair. The delicate curves mostly hidden beneath her station uniform. Those lips that had felt so incredible against Amelia's.

God, she'd been hungry.

Starving, even.

And Simone always seemed to know just what she needed. What other tricks did she have up her sleeve?

13

SIMONE

*T*he inter-office mingle came together a lot quicker than expected.

Everybody was still swamped with work. The firefighters were dedicating all their spare time to cleaning up the city and the ME's office employees were working feverishly to close cases. But that was all the more reason to force everyone to take a break. By the middle of week two, Simone could tell that morale was dangerously low.

"Just because there's work to do and people are dead doesn't mean those of us who are still living don't need to eat and find ways to burn off the stress," she told Amelia when they were on the phone, putting the plans together.

Amelia agreed, so they decided that at lunchtime on Friday, Amelia would gather as many of her employees as she could and bring them to the firehouse. The change of venue had been at Simone's insistence, too.

"I know this was your idea, and you deserve all the

credit," she said. "But you know what would be more fun than eating pizza with the smell of death in the background?"

Amelia laughed. "Anything?"

"Probably," Simone agreed. "Specifically, I was thinking my crew could give yours a firehouse tour. I'll even throw in some training drills—I know some of your people are exercise buffs."

Amelia had agreed that it was a good idea, so they'd ordered a dozen pizzas from a universally loved pizzeria downtown and at noon on Friday, a dozen ME employees flooded into the firehouse. Simone'd had the probies set up tables and chairs, along with a buffet of greasy, delicious lunch foods, and everybody dug right in.

While they were helping themselves, Amelia came to stand by Simone. "Hey. Thanks for having us."

Her eyes flitted momentarily to Simone's lips. She wore a slim-fit pair of black trousers with heels and a silky white blouse, the most form-fitting thing Simone had seen her in so far. On the scene she'd been in coveralls, and the day Simone came to her office, she'd been in scrubs.

Not that she hadn't looked beautiful in both... but she cleaned up nicely too.

"My pleasure," Simone said, thinking of the wet, steamy kiss they'd shared in the downpour and wondering when she'd have another opportunity like that. "I'm glad you came."

"We all definitely needed it," Amelia said. Her crew

was easily mixing with Simone's at the folding tables. "It feels a little like a school field trip."

"If you're good, I'll let you play with the siren in the fire engine," Simone teased.

"Promise?" Amelia asked, her eyes scorching.

Damn, she was gorgeous. If both of their staffs weren't sitting just a few yards away, Simone would wrap her arms around Amelia's tiny waist and kiss her again right then and there.

"Come on, let's get some pizza," she said, to remove the temptation to do just that. "After everybody eats, we'll do the tour."

The two groups mixed and chatted while they ate, and when the pizza boxes were empty—all twelve of them—Simone stood up and gave a quick talk about why she and Amelia had wanted the two departments to meet. She glossed over the part where today was at least a little bit motivated by her desire to find excuses to see Amelia—they didn't need to know that part. Then she broke everybody into two groups.

"If you want a little post-lunch cardio, go with Carter," she said, and he raised his hand so they would know who he was. "He'll show you what we do to stay fit when we're not fighting fires." About five people elected for the high-energy version of events, and Simone said to the rest of them, "Everybody else, come with me and I'll give you the grand tour."

Her probies started to follow her too and Simone gave them a sharp look.

"You three better know your way around here by now," she said. "You get to play janitor. Stay here and clean this mess up."

They retreated back to the lunch tables, and Simone waved everybody else toward the stairs to the second floor. As they walked, Amelia appeared at Simone's elbow, saying, "Well, someone's a stern boss."

"You like that?" Simone asked softly. "Because I can be bossy elsewhere too."

"That's... intriguing," Amelia said, a subtle smile on her lips.

The ideas she was giving Simone was enough to drive her up the wall, but with both their crews around them, this was not the place to start down that line of thought. Better to stick to safe subjects for now.

"Well, you have to make sure new recruits will obey in even mundane situations," she explained. "One of the most important things in an emergency is being able to trust your crew to do what you tell them."

"Makes sense," Amelia nodded. "When my team reports to a scene, they're dealing with death, but your crew faces life-or-death situations."

"The good news is we train constantly for it, even after the probationary period ends," Simone said. "And this batch of probies are significantly less like unruly puppies now... nobody's peed on the rug since Wednesday." That earned her a smile from Amelia. "This week has been one hell of a sink-or-swim situation for them."

"I don't doubt that."

They reached the top of the stairs, where there

was a hallway with a railing on one side and a row of doors on the other. The doors led to sleeping and living quarters that the firefighters used when they were on call, as well as a conference room and kitchen. Simone walked the ME employees through all of it, then invited everybody to look around for themselves.

Amelia stuck close to Simone. The two of them walked lazily up the hallway, and when Simone was sure no one would see, she grazed her finger across the back of Amelia's hand, then lightly over her palm.

"I'm glad you're here."

"I'm glad you forced us all to take a break," Amelia said. "And I've been meaning to find a way to thank you for sending me dinner on Tuesday. You have no idea how much I appreciated it."

Simone smiled. "Well, you already thanked me via text."

"That's not much of a thank you," Amelia said.

Simone shrugged. "If you really feel that it was insufficient, maybe you can let me take you out to an actual restaurant once things settle down a little." Amelia laughed, and it caught her off guard. "What?"

"How is letting *you* take *me* out a way for me to say thanks for the dinner you already bought me?"

Simone smiled. "I've been dying to spend more time with you ever since we met. I don't care who pays—a night out with you is a favor in my book."

"Well, in that case, I accept," Amelia said. "*But* I'm paying. And I have to remind you that, mass disaster or not, I don't have a lot of time for dating. So don't expect this to turn into anything beyond dinner."

"We'll see about that," Simone said. It was a risk, pushing Amelia when she'd clearly stated her boundaries. But there was no way Simone could feel as strongly about Amelia as she did without picking up on the reciprocal emotions Amelia was sending her way. She didn't have a lot of free time? Neither did Simone. It was a challenge she was willing to accept.

She felt her body involuntarily orbiting closer to Amelia's. Yes, if they were alone right now, this moment would definitely end in a kiss. It was a tragedy that it couldn't.

A few of Amelia's people wandered back into the hall and Simone said, "If you want, we can set up a practice drill. My new recruits will show you how fast we have to respond when that alarm goes off, even if we're sound asleep or in the middle of a meal."

"That sounds cool," one of the investigators said.

"Can we go down the fire pole after them?" Jordan asked, pointing to the polished steel pole a few feet away from the stairs.

"You can't come to a firehouse and not use the pole," Simone said. Then she leaned over the railing and called the probies upstairs. She told them to go into the bunk room and pretend to be asleep, then she and Amelia gathered the whole group in the hallway to watch the practice drill. Simone used an airhorn to simulate the fire alarm, shouting, "Fire drill! Go, go, go!"

Velez was the first out of the bunk room, followed by

Williams and then Larson. All three of them had tough-
ened up in the past two weeks, and Simone didn't have
nearly as many reservations about Larson as she did on
day one. The tornado had whipped him into shape faster
than she could have on her own.

The three of them raced down the hall and, one by
one, disappeared down the fire pole to the ground floor.
Everybody watched over the railing as the probies dashed
over to the fire engine and grabbed their protective gear
off hooks nearby. They hustled into heavy coats and
oxygen masks, and they were on the truck in a little over a
minute.

Simone blew the airhorn again and shouted, "Good
job, guys!"

The ME employees clapped for them, then Simone
let them try out the pole. Jordan was the first one down,
whooping the whole way to the floor. A few people took
the stairs, and then it was just Simone and Amelia left on
the landing.

Amelia said, "I guess I better take the stairs—I'm in
heels."

"Do you *want* to try the pole?" Simone asked.

She was standing close to Amelia, closer than she
would have with other people around. But they were all
downstairs now and Simone could see a glimmer of playfulness in Amelia's eyes—a new type of desire that told
Simone the answer. She dropped down to her knees.

"What are you doing?" Amelia asked.

"Raise your foot," Simone said. Amelia did as asked,
and Simone slipped off one heel. "Go down barefoot and

you'll be fine. If you want me to go first and catch you so you don't dirty your socks, I'd be happy to."

Amelia smirked at her. "I bet you would." Then she raised her other foot.

Simone removed the delicate heel. They were Mary Janes, which made it a little easier to hold on to them. She dangled the straps from one finger. "We better get down there or we'll miss all the fun."

"I don't know about that."

Damn, she was being flirty. Simone couldn't wait to take her out to dinner, then see where else the night might take them. "Who do you want to go first?"

"You," Amelia said. "Show me how it's done."

Simone stole a fast kiss, and before Amelia could reprimand her for it, she disappeared through the hole, a grin on her face. She got to the bottom just in time to enjoy the sight of Amelia's slender leg reaching out and wrapping around the pole. Simone set Amelia's shoes on the ground, and as she descended, her blouse billowed up and gave Simone a peek at the supple curves of her satiny bra.

Then Amelia landed in her arms, and Simone helped her to step into her shoes.

"Thank you," Amelia said, her voice breathy and seductive.

Then one of the young women from her office called, "You go, Dr. Trace! I didn't take you for the adventurous type."

Amelia arched an eyebrow in the girl's direction.

"Regardless of how it seems to you, I'm not of hip-breaking age just yet, Reese."

Everybody laughed and the tension melted away. Then Larson, sweating in his protective gear, asked, "What now, Lieu?"

Simone smiled. "Do the drill again. Faster."

14

AMELIA

*A*melia was at her desk the following morning, catching up on the emails that had come in while she and her staff were at the firehouse. It was Saturday, but they were all still working a lot of overtime to process the tornado victims, so she was in the office too.

She'd been whittling down her inbox for about half an hour when her phone rang. It was so rare lately for her to take calls as they came in instead of just answering voicemails that she actually stumbled over her greeting.

"Hello?" Well, that was casual. "Err, this is Dr. Trace."

"Hey, it's Tom."

"What's going on?" Amelia put the phone on speaker, planning to split her attention between the homicide detective and her inbox.

"We got an ID on Jane Doe number eight," he said, and that got her attention.

"Finally."

"She's not local," he said. "That's why it took so long."

"Huh, that's unusual," Amelia said. "So, who is she?"

"Megan Hunter," he said. "A nineteen-year-old student at Granville State University."

"That's at least two hours away," Amelia said. She'd been to medical conferences at that college before, so she was familiar with the area.

"Closer to three," Tom said, "if you're not a speed demon."

Guilty as charged, Amelia thought. Road trips could be so boring, especially when she was in the car by herself. But what was Megan Hunter doing making that drive?

"Do you know what she was doing here?" Amelia asked.

"Not yet," Tom answered. "Her parents filed a missing person report as soon as they legally could. You have to wait seventy-two hours after an adult goes missing, and Megan left Granville early on the morning of the tornado, apparently without telling anyone where she was going."

"And she's got no known ties to this area?" Amelia asked. "No significant other or friends up here?"

"Not that her parents are aware of," Tom said. "Anyway, they're coming up to identify the body on Monday. I told them I'd see what I could do about making sure it was ready to be released then too, so they don't have to make the trip twice."

"Of course," Amelia said. "That shouldn't be a problem."

She made a quick note to herself on a notepad on her cluttered desk, then told Tom what time he should bring the Hunters into the office on Monday. After she hung up, she sat back in her chair for just a minute, imagining how awful it must be to grieve a teenaged child.

It was hard enough just to work on a case like this—she couldn't fathom being a parent in that situation.

Maybe that was part of the reason she'd never settled down, never contemplated the possibility of starting a family of her own. Besides the fact that she hadn't found the right woman, and the weight of her work responsibilities, there was a part of her that was afraid of how much it would hurt to love someone and lose them. She saw it every day at work—it destroyed people.

She took a deep breath, clearing her head. There was work to do and no time for all those twisty, complicated emotions.

*O*n Monday in the late morning, Amelia asked Jordan to bring Megan Hunter's body into the viewing room and make her as presentable as possible for the family. This would be the first time they laid eyes on their daughter since she went missing three weeks ago.

Amelia went out to the lobby so she'd be ready to greet the Hunters when they arrived with Tom, and she pulled her phone out of her back pocket while she waited.

JD #8's family will be here any minute, she texted Simone. *Her name is Megan Hunter.*

Amelia figured she might want to know, since it had been Simone's case too when they were on the scene together. Mostly, though, she was just looking for an excuse to contact her.

They'd been texting ever since they exchanged numbers, but Amelia was swamped with cases and Simone was busy training her new recruits. There hadn't been time to go out like they'd discussed at the firehouse.

Amelia's phone lit up with a reply. *Glad she has a name again, and that she gets to go home.*

Emotion knotted at the base of Amelia's throat but she had to swallow it down when she saw Tom's SUV pull into the parking lot. She stood and tucked her phone away, fixing a muted, sympathetic smile on her face.

The couple that walked with Tom to the front door appeared to be in their mid-fifties. The woman's eyes were glossy and her cheeks were red—she'd clearly been crying recently. The man's lips were pinched tightly together, rigid like the rest of his body.

"Hello, I'm Dr. Trace," Amelia said, extending her hand to each of them. "I'm so sorry for your loss."

"Thank you," the man said stiffly. "I'm Bill Hunter, and this is my wife Nancy." Nancy barely met Amelia's eyes, clutching a balled up tissue. Bill added, "Let's just get this over with, please?"

"Of course."

She led them through the front offices to the viewing room, which was the first room beyond the keypad-locked door dividing the front and back offices. The front could have been any other office building, with groups of cubicles arranged by department. The back was much more clinical and sanitized.

Amelia held the door open and guided the Hunters inside the small room, made even smaller by the hospital curtain hanging from the ceiling to conceal the body until they were ready to see it. There were a couple of chairs and a small end table on their side of the curtain. Tom stepped in behind the Hunters, and Amelia was the last into the room.

Softly, she asked, "Are you ready, Mr. and Mrs. Hunter?"

Nancy leaned against her husband and put one hand to her mouth. Bill spoke for both of them. "Yes."

Amelia drew back the curtain, revealing Megan on a gurney, a white sheet pulled neatly up to her shoulders. Mrs. Hunter immediately burst into fresh tears and Tom automatically reached for a box of tissues that he knew from experience were available on the end table.

"Yes, that's her," Bill said, doing his duty to identify his daughter's body and then turning away.

Amelia reached for the curtain, but Nancy shook her head. "No, leave it open. Can I touch her?"

"Go ahead, Mrs. Hunter," Amelia said, and Tom grabbed her a chair.

The grieving mother grasped her daughter's hand through the sheet and accepted the seat offered to her.

Bill continued to stand toward the back of the room, eyes on the floor.

Amelia had seen just about every reaction a person could have in this room, and these two, although displaying very different grief reactions, were typical. She was about to suggest that she and Tom step out for a couple of minutes when Nancy started to talk.

"Damn it, Megan, why didn't you tell anybody where you were going?"

"She was nineteen, Nance," Bill answered. "She was an adult. She didn't need to tell anyone."

"She always used to tell me everything," Nancy said, turning to Amelia with a look that begged for an explanation, or maybe just empathy. The sympathetic smile she'd honed over the years fell pathetically short of providing actual comfort, and Amelia felt helpless.

"She was growing up," Bill said, "asserting her independence."

"By driving way out here in the middle of a tornado," Nancy said bitterly. "What's in Fox City, anyway?"

At last, her husband seemed to break out of his stupor and he went to her. He put his hand on Nancy's shoulder and said, "That's what the detective is going to find out. Right?"

Tom nodded. "We'll figure this out. I promise."

Amelia said gently, "We'll give you two a moment alone with her. There's a telephone and a list of local funeral homes on the table there if you need them."

Bill shook his head. "She belongs in Granville with

us. We've already made arrangements for her to be picked up."

Amelia nodded. "Okay, good. Well, please let me know if there's anything more I can do for you."

He met her eyes for the first time since they'd come into the office. Light blue just like his wife's, they welled with emotion but Amelia could see he had a stranglehold on it, forcing it to stay just below the surface. "Thank you."

Amelia told them to use the call button near the door when they were finished, then she stepped into the hall and Tom followed, closing the door behind them.

"Could I get a cup of coffee while we wait?" Tom asked.

"Sure," Amelia said. They headed for the break room and Amelia paused with her hand on the door that separated the labs from the office side of the building. She was thinking.

When Tom noticed, he asked, "What's wrong?"

"Did you already talk to the Hunters before you brought them here?" she asked, moving toward the break room again.

Tom nodded. "Yeah, why?"

"Did they say anything about adopting Megan?"

"No, and I didn't exactly think to ask." Tom gave her a probing look. "What are you thinking?"

"Both of the Hunters have blue eyes," Amelia said. "Megan had brown eyes. Genetically speaking, that's exceedingly rare. It's likely that one or both of them are not her biological parents."

"Interesting," Tom said.

They went to the coffee pot and Amelia poured for both of them, then Tom reached for the powdered creamer. Amelia asked, "What color eyes do the Thomases have?"

Tom frowned. "I'll have to check—not something I write down in the normal course of an investigation. You think that's what Megan was doing here, tracking down a biological parent?"

"Maybe," Amelia said. "But you're the homicide detective. That's for you to decide."

He smirked. "I'll ask the Hunters once they're done in the viewing room."

C L A R K

*C*lark was sitting at the kitchen table, a laptop in front of him and his ID card printer to his right.

This was his third new identity, not counting the name on his birth certificate. This time he would be Mark Davis, a generic name he'd pulled from a quick thumb through the phonebook he'd found in the apartment when he moved in.

Before that, he was John Ferguson, which had turned out to be a waste of a perfectly good identity because he'd been entirely too impulsive. He never should have tried to take the girl on that stormy day. He wasn't normally so fast to act. He studied all his potential friends first, got to know them, took his time to make sure they'd be a good match.

But when he picked her up, she was alone and wet, looking desperate, and there was just something about the storm that made Clark lose all his common sense.

She'd only been in his car for about ten minutes, and

when the tornado siren started going off, the whole spontaneous plan went to hell. She ran away from him and he couldn't even remember her name now. But just in case she remembered the one he'd given her, John Ferguson had to die.

At least it had been easy to ditch the car with so much chaos and destruction throughout the city.

Before John, he'd been Eddie Banks. Now, *that* name had served him well, like a lucky charm. It had brought Jenny to him, and before that, AJ and Belle.

Of course, all three of those friendships had soured in the end. He still hadn't figured out how to *keep* the friends he made, but that was why he was trying again now. As his mother always said, if at first you don't succeed, try, try again.

"I'm gonna get it right, Mom," he said to the empty apartment as the completed photo ID popped out of the card printer. Best twenty bucks he'd ever spent at an auction for a school that had been closing.

He held the new card up to the light, scrutinizing it and trying to get used to the name at the same time. The forgery wouldn't convince a cop if he got pulled over, but he knew from experience it was a good enough job to help him create a new rideshare account so he could start over.

"Hi, I'm Mark," he said. "Mark Davis, Mark Davis, Mark Davis."

He'd repeat the new name until it rolled off his tongue automatically. Right now he didn't feel much like a Mark, but he'd never felt like a Clark, either. His mother had always loved it—he was named after Clark Kent, Superman, a legacy he never stood a chance of living up to.

But his mom wasn't around anymore, and neither was Clark. He was Mark now, hopefully forever this time.

He slipped the new ID into his wallet. He needed to make a new rideshare account next, but the ID had taken most of the morning and he was hungry now. That step could wait until after lunch.

He disconnected the printer from his laptop and decided that while he tidied up and made lunch, he would scan the local news sites. He wasn't worried about his latest failed friendship—good luck tracking down John Ferguson—but his mother had taught him to always keep a finger on the pulse of the city. When your bread and butter is illegal—counterfeit money for her, fake identities for him—you need to know what's going on around you.

She'd let down her guard, got cocky, and now she was in jail. That wasn't going to happen to him.

He found a website that was streaming the twelve o'clock news and watched while he tucked the ID printer into a kitchen cabinet with a false back that he'd built just for that purpose. Then he got out bread, lunchmeat and mustard and started assembling a sandwich.

With his back to the table, he listened to the news-caster talking about the week's weather forecast: rain, like they'd been having off and on for weeks now. There was a call for volunteers to help clean up downed tree limbs at a playground, and then something that made Clark forget about his sandwich entirely.

"Have you ever considered whether your rideshare app is safe?" the newscaster asked. "We spoke with one woman who had a harrowing experience during the tornado three weeks ago. Sharon?"

Clark spun around, eyes glued to the laptop screen and his heart climbing into his throat. *Don't let it be her,* he thought, *let it be someone else...*

The newscaster named Sharon was a blonde with 1980s hair, who was sitting on a set made to look like a living room. Across from her was the young woman Clark had picked up the day of the tornado.

Oh, fudge.

He tried to calm his racing pulse by reminding himself that she knew him by an alias he'd already discarded. She'd ridden in a car that he'd abandoned in a bad neighborhood, with the keys in the ignition. She couldn't track him down. If there was a remote chance, he'd have heard from the police by now instead of seeing her on a news show.

Just relax, Clark, err, Mark, he told himself as he sank down into his chair again, pulling the laptop closer to himself.

"You've asked not to be named because your attacker is still at large," Sharon said. "Is that right?"

Clark's would-be friend nodded. "That's right, thank you."

"No, thank *you* for sharing your story," Sharon said.

What a suck-up. Clark rolled his eyes. "Please, tell us what happened."

If there had even been a shadow of a doubt in his mind that this was the same girl he'd picked up, it was obliterated as he listened to her tell her version of events. The chronology and the details were the same—but her perception was all wrong. She told Sharon about the terror she'd experienced, how much danger she'd been in, and not just from the tornado.

How could she misunderstand him so badly? Why did they *all* misunderstand him and fight him until something bad happened?

"He grabbed me... abducted... screamed for help... thought I was going to die." Clark was only partly listening now, but none of the things she was saying made sense and he was stunned to hear her side of the story.

Yes, he knew that his friends wanted to live their own lives. He knew Jenny hadn't wanted to stay in that storage unit and that this girl had resisted when he tried to bring her to an abandoned building he knew of where they could weather the storm. But he also knew better than them.

Jenny had been a drug addict. She needed to detox and the only way it was going to happen was if Clark helped her.

And this girl was too stupid for her own good. She didn't even have the sense to take shelter in the middle of a tornado!

He was *helping* them, damn it.

He was grinding his teeth by the time the interview

ended with Sharon offering up tips for safe ridesharing. It was dumb stuff, like comparing the details on the app to the person who shows up. Stuff that wouldn't have helped any of Clark's friends because he was a legitimate rideshare driver. The news wasn't actually meant to help people—it was entertainment with a side of shock value. Sharon didn't care if her viewers practiced safe rideshare tactics. In fact, it was better for her reporting if bad things kept happening to people.

When Sharon turned things back over to the studio, the anchor asked, "Do the police have any leads on this rideshare imposter?"

"No, it seems he signed up under a false name, and so far there's been no luck tracking down his car," Sharon said. "One good thing is that the rideshare company has been notified and his account has been suspended."

Sure, John Ferguson's has. Clark never actually bothered to check—he just assumed it would be shut down, and even if it wasn't, it would be too dangerous for him to use again. It didn't matter to him at all, though. In a few hours, Mark Davis would be ready to hit the streets.

He'd just have to be more careful this time, choose his friends more wisely and take his time.

He'd get it right eventually.

SIMONE

*A*t the end of week three, post-tornado, things around Fox City were finally starting to feel normal again. Simone had headed up the playground clean-up project that was one of the last items on her firehouse's to-do list, and between the probies and an army of volunteers who'd showed up, it hadn't taken long at all.

Of course, those who had lost loved ones, personal property, their homes, were on a much longer path back to normalcy.

But at least things weren't feeling so grim anymore. The sun had even started to shine again after a very long rainy stretch. That was what inspired Simone to call Amelia in the evening when the playground clean-up was complete.

"What are you doing tonight?" she asked when Amelia picked up.

"Nothing so far, but I have a feeling you're about to change that."

"Only if you're up for it," Simone said. "I know you've been crazy busy at work, but I do have an idea to help you blow off some steam."

"I like the sound of that," Amelia answered, and Simone grinned.

She'd seen the playfulness in Amelia's eyes when they were at the firehouse and Simone had coaxed her down the fire pole. Amelia may have put up a fight at first and objected on the grounds of her wardrobe, but there was a little kid inside her begging to come out and play. And that was exactly what Simone had in mind.

"What time do you get off work?" she asked.

"In half an hour," Amelia said. "What are we doing?"

"It's a surprise," Simone said. "Wear something casual, pants. And no heels."

They arranged for Simone to pick Amelia up at her place at six. That gave Simone the perfect amount of time to go back to her apartment, shower and change into something a little less utilitarian than her station uniform. She ended up in a pair of jeans and a V-neck tee, with an olive-green bomber jacket draped over her arm just in case it got cold.

She drove over to the address Amelia texted her, which turned out to be a classic-looking two-story farmhouse in a suburban neighborhood. It was a far cry from the ten-story apartment building Simone lived in within walking distance of the firehouse, and it reminded her of their ten-year age gap. Not that it was a bad thing—Simone had dated women who were younger than herself, who did not have their shit together, and she wasn't looking for that kind of drama anymore.

She just hoped that Amelia was into whatever drama Simone brought into her life.

She pulled up the drive and rang the doorbell. When Amelia answered, she was in a striped T-shirt and a pair of khaki shorts, looking elegant and gorgeous as always. Simone took her hand, then pulled Amelia closer. She wrapped one arm around the small of her back and greeted her with a kiss.

"I've been wanting to do that for an eternity," she sighed when the kiss ended.

"I'm glad you did," Amelia answered. "So, am I dressed appropriately?"

"You look perfect," Simone said, offering Amelia her arm. They walked down the sidewalk to her car, and once they got back on the road, Simone commented, "That's some house you've got."

Amelia's cheeks colored. "It's too much house, honestly. I love it, but I don't think I would have chosen it for myself."

A little surge of jealousy rose in Simone's belly as she imagined Amelia with some other woman, in some past life, house shopping and settling on that farmhouse. "Did a previous partner choose it?"

Amelia laughed and shook her head. "No, nothing like that. It's the house I grew up in. When my parents passed, they willed it to my sister and me. We both agreed that we couldn't bring ourselves to put it up for sale, and since I still live in the area and my sister doesn't, I bought her out."

"Oh, I'm sorry about your parents," Simone said. "How long ago did they pass?"

"It's been about ten years now," Amelia said. "Dad went first, his heart, and Mom passed a few years later. I think she missed him too much."

"That's morbidly sweet," Simone said. "They were deeply in love, huh?"

"Yeah, my sister and I were lucky to have them as an example. She's happily married now, and I'm married to my work," Amelia laughed. "Tell me about your family."

Simone snorted. "Nothing so fairy-tale as that. My folks divorced when I was in middle school. Mom moved away, I talk to her a few times a year. Dad still lives in the area, and he's remarried now. He's happy."

"That's good. Siblings?"

"Just me."

"Sometimes I wished to be an only child when I was younger," Amelia admitted. "Little sisters are such a pain in the ass. But we get along well now. Anyway, where are we going?"

Simone smiled wide. "I had a sort of corny idea, but I hope you'll like it."

"I like corny," Amelia promised.

Simone told her about the clean-up efforts at the playground, and by the time she finished explaining, they'd arrived. It was dusk, the new saplings the volunteers had planted just visible in the diminishing light, and

Simone parked on the street to avoid drawing attention to themselves.

"Full disclosure," she said as she opened Amelia's car door for her, "the playground closes at sunset so we're *technically* doing something illegal. If you're not feeling like a rebel tonight, we can go to a restaurant and have a more conventional date."

Amelia took Simone's hand as she stepped out of the car, and didn't let go. Her skin was soft and warm, and there was a glimmer in her eyes. "Let's walk on the wild side."

"Are you sure?" Simone teased. "I wouldn't want to be a bad influence."

"I think it's a little late for that," Amelia said. Then she released Simone's hand and took off running. "Last one down the slide's a rotten egg!"

Simone laughed and gave chase. While Amelia scrambled up a rope ladder and headed for the top of the slide, Simone took a shortcut and ran up the bottom of it. They met in the middle, where Simone planted a sloppy kiss on Amelia and promptly lost her footing. Amelia shrieked and grabbed her, and they somehow made it to the bottom with life and limb intact.

"Let me guess, when you were little, you were the kid with perpetually skinned knees who was always trying to do a three-sixty loop on the swings," Amelia said with a laugh.

"Nailed it," Simone said. "And now I run into burning buildings for a living, so I guess I haven't changed all that much." She was in no hurry to get off the slide and out of Amelia's arms. "What about you? What were you like as a kid?"

"Guess."

"Hmm..." Simone trailed one finger up Amelia's thigh, over her shorts and up to her waist. "I bet you were the kid who brought a book to recess."

She dug her fingers into Amelia's side, tickling her. Amelia squirmed beneath her, body pressing against Simone's in a dozen tantalizing ways.

"Well?" Simone asked, not letting up on the tickles but demanding an answer anyway. "Am I right?"

"Yes, yes!" Amelia relented in gasps that bordered on not-playground-friendly. That sound was giving Simone ideas for the rest of the evening, but before she could comment on them, Amelia tore out of her arms and popped to her feet. "Come on, I'll push you on the swing set. We'll get you over the top bar."

She grabbed Simone's hand, pulling her to her feet. Simone laughed. "It's not possible."

"Maybe not," Amelia said. "But we gotta try."

They took the monkey bars over to the swings, and it was really a treat to see Amelia completely let go of her serious, professional working woman persona. The more they played, the younger and happier she seemed, and pride swelled in Simone's belly at knowing she was the cause.

Neither of them ended up making a complete loop on the swings, despite their best efforts. It was still, tragically, an impossibility according to the laws of physics. Once they'd tired themselves out trying, they ended up swinging lazily next to each other and just talking. Eventually, the conversation turned to work.

"I talked to Tom earlier today," Amelia said. "There's news on the Megan Hunter case."

"Her family took her home, right?" Simone asked. "And you had Tom look into something to do with her eye color?"

Amelia had been keeping Simone in the loop whenever her schedule allowed, although all that stuff about genetics and recessive genes and alleles that Amelia had tried to explain to her had gone over her head. She'd learned all that in high school biology, then promptly forgot it once the class was over.

"He had a hunch based on how they were acting in the viewing room that if Bill Hunter *wasn't* Megan's father, he might not know it," Amelia explained, "so he made an excuse to speak to Nancy alone and asked her."

"What did she say?"

"She got pregnant in her final semester of college, and even though she was monogamous with Bill when they were dating, they'd broken up over the winter break and there had been another guy," Amelia said. "Bill popped the question when he found out, and she knew she wanted to marry him so she never told him."

"Does she know which man is the father?" Simone asked.

Amelia shook her head. "Get this: she doesn't even know the name of the other guy. They met at a party and she never saw him again. But guess who has brown eyes?"

"Cal Thomas," Simone said.

Amelia looked impressed. "You could be a detective."

"My talents are in the firehouse," Simone said. "But a lot of people have brown eyes. I do."

Amelia nodded. "Tom's working on covertly acquiring DNA from Cal to do a paternity test. If he's her father, we'll know why she was at his house that morning."

"Do you think he knew about her?" Simone wondered.

"He claimed he didn't recognize her," Amelia pointed out.

"It wouldn't be out of the question to lie about something like that, though," Simone argued back. "Your whole house gets ripped apart, you probably don't want your wife and kid finding out that you have another child on the same day."

"True, but Nancy Hunter seemed pretty motivated to keep her own husband from finding out," Amelia said. "I bet she kept that secret pretty closely guarded."

"Well, it wouldn't be the first time in the history of the world that a woman got pregnant and decided the father wasn't dad material," Simone said. She reached across the swings and took Amelia's hand, squeezing it. "Okay, that's enough depressing shit for our first date. Push me across the zipline and we'll find out if I exceed the weight limit."

A couple hours and a takeout meal later, Amelia and Simone wound up back at the farmhouse.

They'd gotten a little frisky on the playground, resisting the urge to push too far past light, flirtatious kisses and sensual embraces. It may have been closed after dark, but it *was* still a playground. But Simone had barely taken her eyes away from Amelia since their date began, and the better she got to know Simone, the more Amelia wanted to rescind her no-dating policy.

There had to be a way to make it work, right? Other people had demanding careers *and* successful love lives. Amelia had rejected that for herself while she was busy climbing the ladder at the ME's office, but it didn't have to be that way forever, did it?

They went inside and Amelia led Simone to the kitchen. They had pasta from one of her favorite Italian places—Amelia had paid, as she'd insisted the other day in the firehouse—but they both had something other than food on their minds.

"Do you want a quick tour before we eat?" Amelia asked.

"I'd love that," Simone said. She was standing very close to Amelia, and their bodies kept brushing against each other accidentally-on-purpose.

The house was decorated in a mix of Amelia's own tastes and the furniture and décor that her parents had collected over a lifetime here. The result was cozy and a little cluttered, but warm. She felt comfortable here, but the house was much too large for one person.

"I keep thinking I should get a pet," Amelia said as she led Simone through the living room. "There's a big backyard that would be perfect for a dog."

"Why don't you get one?" Simone asked.

"I'm hardly ever home," Amelia answered. "Plus, it's the same reason I don't date—there's no time."

"I bet you could find some time if you really wanted to," Simone said with a wink. She was persistent when she set her sights on something she wanted, and it was one of the things Amelia admired about her.

"Come on, I'll show you the upstairs," Amelia said. Her cheeks were burning and her core had been aching ever since the playground. That had been like one long foreplay session, teasing each other, touching each other but just barely. It had been years since Amelia felt this strongly about anyone, and now that Simone was in her house, she was confident that neither of them actually cared about the takeout they'd bought—at least not right now.

Amelia took Simone's hand in her own and led the way. Simone's thumb brushed over the back of her hand while they walked, and that small gesture sent a delicious tingle all through Amelia's body. She wanted more of it.

"Here's my bedroom," she said when they got to the first door in the upstairs hallway.

There were quite a few bedrooms here—more than her family of four had ever needed—and now three of them stood empty except for when Frannie and her husband came to visit.

Amelia had moved into the master suite when she took over the house, and she led Simone into it. The room was spacious and airy, with white walls and lots of light during the day. Right now, it was pitch dark so Amelia switched on a bedside lamp, casting the room in a warm glow and sending shadows up the walls.

"What do you think?" she asked, gesturing to the room.

"It's very 'you,'" Simone told her. "Practical but cozy, and it makes me want to stay a while. I'd love to take a closer look at the bed, though."

Amelia laughed, but in an instant, Simone had closed the gap between them and stolen her breath right out of her lungs. She kissed Amelia passionately, her hands finding Amelia's hips. The playground had been fun, and it was sweet that Simone kept trying to find ways to make Amelia take breaks and relax. But this right here? This was all she'd really wanted since the day they met.

They both lost themselves to the moment, giving in to the desires that had been building between them until they'd grown palpable.

Simone's fingers came to the hem of Amelia's shirt, tugging it up and gently over her head. Then she dropped to her knees and pressed a kiss to Amelia's stomach. Her fingertips trailed along the lines of Amelia's abdomen and brushed the waistband of her shorts.

She unbuttoned them and peeled them down Amelia's thighs, her breath warm against Amelia's belly. She put one hand on Simone's shoulder as she stepped out of her pants, and Simone seized the opportunity to hook Amelia's thigh and lift it onto her shoulder, pressing a kiss to Amelia's sex through the thin fabric of her panties. Her lips felt warm and tantalizing, making heat waves ripple through Amelia's body.

She was unwrapping Amelia like the most precious gift, taking her time and truly savoring every moment of it. It was unlike anything Amelia had ever experienced before. When was the last time she'd slowed down to truly savor *anything,* let alone a beautiful woman? She was so used to focusing on her destination, getting there so she could move on to something else.

It wasn't like that with Simone, in the bedroom or any other part of her life. She lived in the moment and was present in every minute of her life. Every time Amelia was with her, it felt like time stood still and she got to live like that too. Maybe that was how they could be together —all they needed to do was stop time.

When she was in just her bra and panties, Amelia

took Simone by the hand and lifted her back up to her feet. "I think you're overdressed."

Simone was in a pair of jeans and a thin T-shirt, and Amelia undressed her not quite as carefully as Simone had done, but just as enthusiastically. Then they lay down together on the bed, their bodies entwined and their hands exploring each other. Simone ran her fingers through Amelia's hair, pulling it out of its ponytail and letting it go wild across the pillow.

Amelia kissed the plump tops of Simone's breasts spilling over her bra, then brought both hands up to the silky cups. Simone let out a small groan of pleasure that turned into a growl, then pounced on Amelia, grabbing her by both wrists and pinning her to the mattress.

"You always have to be in control and in charge, Dr. Trace," she said, her eyes locked on Amelia's. "Well, not tonight. Tonight, you are mine to play with, mine to pleasure."

Amelia struggled against Simone, mostly just as an excuse to move her hips against Simone's core. Her eyelids fluttered shut for a moment, telling Amelia she'd hit the right spot, but she kept her grip on Amelia's wrists. She wasn't going to relent.

Simone bent down, nuzzling the crook of Amelia's neck. She dragged her tongue along Amelia's flesh, all the way up to her ear, making her shiver and squirm. "Do you like that?"

Amelia had no words. All she could do was nod.

Simone released one wrist to stroke down Amelia's stomach. Her fingers hooked into Amelia's panties and she sucked in a breath, anticipating the touch that would come next. Simone paused, making her ache for it, and Amelia arched her back, pressing her hips against Simone's body.

"Touch me," she breathed. "I want you so bad."

"God, I want you too," Simone groaned, sliding one leg between Amelia's thighs as she settled beside her. She moved her hips, grinding against Amelia's clit and watching the pleasure bloom across her face. "I've thought about this a lot in the last few weeks."

"Me too," Amelia said. "You've got me so close already."

"I want to taste you," Simone whispered, pressing her lips to Amelia's and then sliding her tongue into her mouth. Between kisses, she said, "I want to fuck you until you can't remember your name."

The words made Amelia's body flush with desire, need rippling through her. Simone dragged her panties down her thighs, and quickly dispensed with her own. Then she lay back down beside Amelia, one leg thrown over her thigh, Simone's pussy wet against Amelia's hip. Her hand went to Amelia's bare sex and her knees fell open. She couldn't remember the last time she'd been this wet for anyone.

Simone did something special to her. She'd never felt such an instant attraction to another woman, and just thinking of Simone, or seeing her name pop up on her phone when they texted, was enough to make her core hot and her chest full.

Simone's fingers slid through the slick folds of her

pussy and glided over her clit. Amelia's thighs shook and she knew it wouldn't be long before she was coming against Simone's hand.

"I have one demand," Amelia said, grabbing Simone's wrist and stilling her hand before she could go any further.

Simone cocked an eyebrow at her. "I thought I told you to relax and let me make you feel good."

"You did." Amelia's eyes were locked on Simone's and she didn't back down.

Simone smiled. "What do you want?"

"Your hot pussy, sitting on my face," Amelia said, and Simone bit her lip.

"Goddamn, I was wrong—you're hot when you make demands."

"I want us to come together," Amelia said. "I want to taste you too."

Simone kissed her deeply, inhaling her, one hand going to Amelia's hip and squeezing hard. She could feel just how much Simone wanted her, and the feeling was definitely mutual.

Then Simone let go and turned to face the foot of the bed. Amelia scooted downward and Simone straddled her head. She lay down, their bellies meeting and her full breasts against Amelia's hips. Then she dropped her mouth to Amelia's clit with such urgency that she couldn't help crying out and digging her fingernails into Simone's thighs.

"Oh my God," she gasped. If Simone was going to eat

her pussy like that, she wouldn't have the concentration, or even the muscle control, to return the favor.

"You're even sexier in real life than in my fantasies," Simone murmured, her lips vibrating against Amelia's clit.

Before she lost herself completely, Amelia lifted her head and buried her face in Simone's dripping pussy, lapping and sucking at her. The banter stopped as they both absorbed themselves in the moment, and it wasn't long before Simone's thighs were shaking against Amelia's ears.

"I'm gonna come," Simone groaned, two fingers pressing at Amelia's entrance.

"Come for me," Amelia urged. "Fuck me and come with me."

She had both arms wrapped around the dip in Simone's lower back, tonguing her clit and her entrance. She felt Simone's fingers plunge into her, and a moment later, they were both coming hard, everything in the world fading to black except their two bodies pressed tight against each other, moving as one.

*S*imone stayed the night. They reheated their takeout dinners for a late-night snack, then retreated to the bedroom because neither of them could get enough of each other. And when they were both exhausted and content, Amelia pulled the sheet up around them and Simone cradled Amelia in the curve of her arm.

"This okay?" she asked.

"It's perfect," Amelia had answered. If only they really had found a way to freeze time, to hit pause on all her responsibilities and just be with each other. At least they had tonight.

Just before she drifted off, Amelia asked softly, "Simone? You awake?"

"Hmm?" She sounded half-alert at best, and she held Amelia a little more tightly. It felt perfect.

"Remember when I said I didn't have time to date?"

"Yeah."

"I wish I did," Amelia said.

"Me too."

"Maybe I can find time, as long as you're okay with the fact that I work long hours and I have to prioritize my job."

Simone kissed the top of her head. "Babe, I'm a firefighter. I'm in the exact same boat."

"What if that means we *never* have time for each other?"

"We found time tonight," Simone pointed out. "Why don't we just agree to try, and see what happens?"

Amelia nodded, loving the way Simone's breast felt against her cheek as she snuggled up to her. "I'd like that."

It was the last thought she had before she drifted off to sleep. She spent the rest of the night curled up against Simone, not moving an inch, and it was the most restful sleep she'd had in ages—even better than that bubble bath she'd been dreaming of since the tornado.

---

*I*n the morning, Amelia woke to sun streaming in the window and an aching bladder. She gently wormed her way out from under Simone's arm and tiptoed into the bathroom, then went downstairs to start brewing some coffee. It was still early —she wanted to go into the office and chip away at her paperwork, but that didn't have a deadline, and Simone had mentioned that she had a shift today but not until the afternoon.

When Amelia came back upstairs with two cups of coffee, some cream and sugar and a couple of breakfast croissants on a tray, Simone was still sleeping peacefully. She'd turned her face into Amelia's pillow and her lips were curled into a slight smile—hopefully she was having sweet dreams.

Amelia decided to set the breakfast tray down on the bedside table and let Simone sleep while she took a shower. But as soon as she set the tray down, her phone started ringing in the pocket of her robe.

Loudly.

"Damn," she muttered, hurrying to silence the ringer.

She was too slow though. Simone's eyes popped open and she sat up. For a second she looked alarmed, trying to place her surroundings, and then she relaxed. She smiled at Amelia. "Any time I wake up to an alarm, my first thought is that I'm at the station and there's a fire. Good morning."

"Good morning." She smiled back, then remembered the phone and looked at the screen. "It's Tom."

"Don't take it, you're not working today," Simone begged, reaching for her, but they both knew that wasn't going to happen.

Amelia answered the phone. "Tom, what's happening?"

"Aww, shit, it's Saturday," he said in lieu of a greeting. "Sorry to bug you."

"No, it's fine," she said. "Can I do something for you?"

"Nothing, that's why I feel like a dick for calling so early," he said. "I just wanted to give you an update on the Megan Hunter case."

"What's going on?" She put the phone on speaker and sat down beside Simone so she could listen in.

"I'm still waiting on the DNA results from Cal Thomas—you know how slow the labs are, especially at the end of the week," he said. "But I did hear back from a detective friend I reached out to in Granville. Guess who has a registered nine-millimeter and doesn't know where it is?"

Amelia frowned, and Simone's mouth popped open.

"One of Megan's parents," Simone guessed.

"Olivier, is that you?" Tom asked.

Simone put a hand over her mouth and looked at Amelia, then lowered her hand to whisper, "*Sorry.*"

Tom just laughed though. "I *knew* you two had a

thing. Anyway, you got the nail on the head—Bill Hunter has a nine-mil, and when I called to ask him about it, he checked his gun safe and said it's gone missing."

"He didn't know it was missing until you asked?" Amelia answered.

"I have a feeling he knew once I told him about the bullet wound on Monday, but he probably didn't want to say anything because it makes Megan look bad, stealing her dad's gun," Tom said. "I'm going down there today to talk to the Hunters face-to-face. Just figured you'd want to know."

"Thanks, Tom," Amelia said. Then, thinking of what happened last time he traveled for work, she added, "Be safe."

He promised he would, then hung up the phone. Amelia put hers back in the pocket of her robe, and Simone wondered aloud, "Why would Megan bring a gun to meet her bio-dad?"

"And how did she get shot with it?" Amelia added. Then she pointed to the tray on the bedside table. "I brought you breakfast. I'm going to get a quick shower."

Simone caught her hand before she could get up from the bed. "How about I come with you and we make it a slow shower instead?"

"I like the sound of that," Amelia said. In fact, she liked everything about her first date with Simone, and she was starting to think it was just what she needed.

18

SIMONE

*S*imone hadn't expected to spend the night with Amelia. All she'd really wanted to get out of their date was to get to know her a little better and make sure Amelia took a little time to decompress when she'd been working so hard amid the mass disaster.

Instead, it felt like she'd spent the last eight hours falling in love.

It was surreal, and when at last Amelia decided it was time to go into the office and get some work done, Simone asked, "Can we do this again soon?"

"We better," Amelia said, and the immediacy of her response made Simone's heart flutter with joy. Amelia had been so insistent over the last few weeks that she had no time to date, but Simone knew all she needed to do was wear her down. It looked like she'd been successful.

"Breakfast tomorrow morning?" Simone asked.

Amelia laughed. "After your shift?"

"Yeah," Simone said. "Meet me at that little place by

the police precinct. All the cops I know swear by it, and you know they know their breakfast foods."

"I'm looking forward to it," Amelia promised. They kissed at the door, starting with a sweet goodbye and soon morphing into something much deeper and more urgent. At last, Amelia nudged Simone's shoulder away. "We have to stop or I'm going to drag you back into my bed for the rest of the day."

"Would that be such a bad thing?" Simone asked.

*W*hen Simone reported to the firehouse that evening, she was still walking on air, her head full of Amelia's scent, her body remembering the feeling of her curves pressed up against her.

And then Carter yanked her right out of her reverie and brought her back down to earth. "Wow, I think somebody got lucky last night."

"What?" Suddenly self-conscious, Simone wondered if she had love bites on her neck or something. She looked around, and half her crew was staring at her, probies included. "Mind your business, guys."

For once, nobody seemed interested in listening to their lieutenant's orders. Carter persisted, and that seemed to give everyone else permission to listen in. "I swear I've never seen a dopey smile like that on your face. Who's the lucky lady?"

"She seemed pretty familiar with that medical examiner the day of the tornado," Williams suggested, and

Simone's mouth dropped open. She really was losing her touch if the probies thought they could speculate about her love life like that.

"You know what else would make me smile?" she asked. "Seeing the fire engine cleaned up and detailed. Williams, Larson, Velez, give it a good wash. And Carter, if you make another crack about my love life, you'll be waxing it from bumper to bumper."

He may have been her best friend at the station, but she wasn't about to let him compromise her professional image in front of half the crew. Suddenly she understood exactly what Amelia had been talking about when it came to staying on top in a male-dominated field. You had to be on your guard all the time, and your love life could easily become a weakness—but only if you let it.

Simone pointed the probies in the direction of the supply closet so they could get started, then headed upstairs to clock in and grab a snack. She'd burned a whole lot of calories in the last twenty-four hours, and some late-night pasta and a croissant weren't enough to replace them.

Carter appeared in the kitchen as she was rooting around in a cupboard. "Hey, sorry I called you out."

Simone came up with a protein bar and took it over to the dining table. They both sat and she said, "You know how hard I work to be taken seriously around here."

"Yeah, you're a total hard ass," Carter teased.

"Just don't tease me about Amelia in front of people, okay?" she said. "I'm not just another one of the guys anymore and I need them to see me as their lieutenant."

"Got it," Carter said. Then he grinned. "Amelia—that's the cougar-y coroner, right?"

Simone wrinkled her nose. "Okay, rule number two, never refer to her as a cougar again. In fact, you just keep her out of your filthy head, okay?"

Carter laughed. "You really like her."

I do, Simone thought. Nobody else put a smile on her face the way Amelia did, and Simone usually didn't mind sharing the details of her hook-ups with Carter. But Amelia was so much more than a hook-up, and Simone wanted to hoard all the precious details of their night together, keeping them for herself because they were special.

Apparently, Carter didn't need more of a response than the emotion written on Simone's face. He turned earnest, saying, "It's about time. I'm happy for you."

It was a sweet moment, which Simone ended by blowing raspberries at him. Then the fire alarm started to ring, and they both jumped to their feet.

"It's go time," she said, shoving the protein bar in her pocket. She and Carter ran down the hall to the fire pole, and when they got to the ground floor, she shouted to the probies, "Forget the cleaning, get into your gear!"

Ten minutes later, the fire engine pulled to a stop in front of an apartment building with smoke billowing out of its third-story windows. Simone jumped off the rig along with the rest of her crew and surveyed the scene while the probies uncoiled the hose.

"Hey, where's the hydrant wrench?" Velez called.

"Oh no," Williams groaned. "I think I left it at the Balch Street hydrant."

All three of them looked to Simone, who rolled her eyes. "There's a spare in that compartment."

She pointed to the side of the truck, then made a mental note to go back to Balch Street when she had the time and see if she could find the wrench. It wasn't that they were all that expensive, but people—teenagers in particular—just loved to open up hydrants in the summer and a wrench lying on the ground right beside it would be too much of a temptation.

While the probies connected the hose to a nearby hydrant, Simone jogged over to a cop who'd responded to the scene. It was Mel Pine, who Simone had met on scenes a few times before. She asked, "What's the story?"

"A neighbor from across the street saw smoke and called it in to dispatch," Mel said. "There are ten apartments in the building, but the good news is everybody had already evacuated themselves by the time I arrived. I'm waiting on paramedics for a couple of them due to smoke inhalation."

She gestured to a young couple sitting on the curb, their arms around each other. They coughed periodically, but otherwise seemed fine. The rest of the building residents were all huddled together on the sidewalk, watching the spectacle and hoping their apartments wouldn't burn.

"You sure the building is clear?" Simone asked.

Mel said, "I haven't gone in, but everybody who was home tonight is accounted for."

Simone gathered her crew and gave them the game plan. The fire looked like it was contained on the third floor, and if they acted fast, they could save the rest of the building. She directed Larson and Velez to open the hydrant while she sent Carter up the fire engine ladder with the hose over his shoulder to start dousing the fire. He'd only climbed halfway up when a woman shrieked behind Simone.

"My baby!" the woman screamed as she ran up the sidewalk. "Oh God, Julie!"

She was heading straight for the burning building and Simone caught her by the wrist before she could go inside. "Ma'am, you can't go in there. Your baby is inside?"

Talk about every firefighter's nightmare.

Tears streaked down the woman's cheeks and Simone registered the scrub uniform she wore, the Fox County Hospital ID badge clipped to her breast pocket. "I was at work," the woman said. "I got called in to cover a shift this afternoon and I couldn't get a babysitter. It was just for a few hours!"

Simone asked, "How old is Julie?"

"Nine," the woman sobbed, and relief washed over Simone. At least they weren't talking about a literal baby. The woman insisted, "I have to go in there!"

"You can't be in the building, it's not safe," Simone said. She was having trouble holding the woman back and she waved Velez over to help. Together, they guided the woman a safe distance away and sat her down on the curb. Then Simone told Velez, "Go ask around among the residents. See if you can find her daughter."

"On it," Velez said, then jogged away. In the three weeks she'd been working with Simone, she always brought her A game, she never disobeyed orders, and Simone was starting to really trust her. The other two probies were making progress too, but Simone could already tell that Velez would make a great firefighter.

Simone turned back to the woman, trying to keep her calm. "What's your name, ma'am?"

"H-Helen," she stammered. "I know nine's too young to stay home alone, but it was just for a few hours after school, and just this once. I don't have anybody else to help out, there was no one to watch her..."

She was rambling now, and Simone did her best to soothe her. That only lasted a few seconds, because Velez came running back over and said, "None of the neighbors saw Julie come out of the building."

Simone turned back to Helen. "Are you *sure* Julie was home this afternoon? She didn't go over to a friend's house or stay late at school?"

Helen shook her head, trying to get to her feet again. "She would have texted me if she had. Julie!"

Simone pushed her back down to the sidewalk and told Velez, "Keep her out of the building." Then, turning to Helen, she promised, "I'll find your daughter. Which apartment is yours?"

"Three-oh-six," Helen said.

Oh shit, Simone thought. She looked up at the third floor, where flames were actually licking the exterior of the brick at a couple of the windows.

The strange sense of calm that always enveloped Simone when she was right in the middle of a high-stakes situation descended, and she called two of her most senior crewmembers over. Carter was still on the ladder, spraying water into the windows where the fire was concentrated, and Simone radioed up to him to let him know they were going in. Then she donned her face mask and turned her oxygen on.

Inside, the air in the stairwell of the first two floors was dark and hazy, warmer than it should have been for sure, but not too bad. It wasn't until they were halfway up the flight to the third floor that the heat really cranked up.

Even in all that heavy gear, Simone felt it. She could tell the air quality was bad, and there was a lot more smoke in the hallway on floor three.

"Everybody get down low," she said, her voice muffled through her mask. "Apartment 306. Split up and search, but stay in communication."

"Got it, Lieu."

The door handle to 306 was hot, and locked. Simone kicked it open and stepped aside as black smoke billowed out. This was definitely the source of the fire. She dropped to her knees and crawled into the apartment, her crew right behind her.

"Julie?" she called. "We're firefighters—we're here to help you."

There was no answer, but she wasn't sure she'd be able to hear it if there had been. The fire was so close now it was loud, snapping and gnawing at the wood walls. They needed to get out of there, fast.

"Julie!" she called again, crawling from the living room into what she hoped was the girl's bedroom. "Where are you?"

If they couldn't find her–

Simone forced herself to stop thinking like that. They *would* find her, and then they'd get out of this building before the whole thing came down.

"Kitchen's engulfed," she heard one of her guys call from behind her. "No girl, though."

"Bathroom's clear," another said.

The bedroom Simone was in had light pink walls and a lot of stuffed animals. It was definitely a little girl's room, a likely place for Julie to seek comfort if she was home alone when the fire started.

Unfortunately, it also appeared to share a wall with the kitchen. As Simone inched deeper into the room, she felt an intense heat coming from the shared wall, and curls of black smoke were snaking from the electrical outlets.

Simone crawled over to the twin bed in the middle of the room and lifted a frilly pink bed skirt. A pair of glistening blue eyes, wide and terrified, looked out at her from under the bed. The girl shrank back, a reaction Simone was used to, especially when she was in her gear.

"It's okay," she said, lifting her mask so Julie could see her face. "I'm a firefighter."

146

"Mommy..." Julie whined, scooting deeper beneath the bed.

They didn't have much time. Simone inched a little closer and said as gently as she could, "Hi, honey, I'm Simone. Your mom's downstairs waiting for you. Can I take you to her?"

She held out her hand. The girl hesitated, and Simone resisted the urge to reach in and drag her out. This would go easier if the girl wasn't terrified of her, but if it came to that, Simone would haul her out of here.

Luckily, Julie took her hand.

Simone helped her crawl out from under the bed, then she held the mask up to her. "Will you put this on for me? It's really smoky out there and this will help you breathe."

Julie nodded and Simone put the mask over her face. It was much too big, but better than nothing. Simone picked the girl up in her arms, then carried her out to the living room.

"I've got her," she called to her guys. "Come on, let's get out of here!"

The act of shouting brought hot smoke into her lungs and she started coughing. Julie wrapped her arms around Simone's neck, scared, and as soon as Simone had eyes on both her crewmembers, she headed for the door.

The air in the hallway was even denser than before, acrid and unbreathable. Simone ran down the stairs with the girl in her arms and her crew at her heels. She tried not to inhale, tried not to need air. There were too many stairs, though, too far to go. When she breathed, the hot, toxic air sliced at her lungs and made her cough violently.

"Lieu," one of the guys called from behind her. "Take my mask."

"We're almost there," she answered. She'd been trained to make sure her crew was safe, to think of them and the people she was rescuing and put herself last.

When they emerged from the building, the night air felt like ice-cold heaven. She dropped to her knees and let go of the little girl as Helen shrieked, "Julie!"

"Mommy!"

Simone helped Julie take off the mask, and her last thought as she watched the little girl run into her mother's arms was that she needed oxygen. She should put the mask back on her own face, breathe deep.

Instead, the world went black as she collapsed.

19

AMELIA

*I*t was early on Sunday morning when Amelia got a call from an unknown number. She was in the bathroom getting ready to meet Simone at the diner and she nearly let it go to voicemail, figuring it was some particularly unscrupulous telemarketer. But something told her to answer.

"Hi, Amelia, this is Carter from the firehouse. Do you remember me?" A man said when she picked up.

"Yes, is everything okay?" Amelia's gut immediately felt heavy, like there was a large stone in it.

"Simone's in the hospital," he said, then hurried to add, "she's okay."

"What happened?" Amelia demanded, sinking down on the edge of the bathtub to listen.

"We got called out to an apartment fire," he said. "She sustained some pretty severe smoke inhalation. Paramedics took her to the hospital around seven o'clock and kept her overnight for observation. They're going to

149

release her sometime this morning and she asked me to call you."

"Thank you," Amelia said, her voice shaky.

"She saved a nine-year-old girl," Carter added. "She's a hero."

"I already know that," Amelia answered.

A handful of conflicting emotions swirled in Amelia's chest. Part of her wanted to go to Simone right that second and never let her go. Another part was afraid that this was what life with a firefighter would be like. Her own job was demanding, but it wasn't dangerous. Did she have what it took to open up her heart to someone who ran into burning buildings for a living and put her own life at risk on a regular basis?

In the end, there was only one thing she needed to know. "What hospital is she in?"

"Fox County," Carter said. "Her dad and stepmom are coming, but I know she wants to see you too."

"Thank you."

"And don't worry too much—Lieu's tough, she's been through worse."

Amelia was sure that was meant to be comforting, but it only made her wonder what *worse* meant. How often did this happen?

But she cared about Simone more than she was scared for herself, and she needed to see her. She thanked Carter again and hung up the phone. Thirty minutes later, she was at the hospital, looking for an employee to point her in the right direction.

"Are you family?" the woman she found at the reception desk asked.

For a split second, Amelia thought about lying just to make sure she'd be able to get in to see Simone. They'd only known each other three weeks and already she was willing to lie to get to her. But she shook her head and explained, "No, I'm a colleague and... a friend."

More than that, she was sure Simone would agree. But they hadn't actually discussed it yet so she stuck with 'friend.'

Amelia wasn't willing to lie to get to Simone, but she didn't mind pulling rank to see if she could get a little more information. She added, "I'm also a doctor. Can you tell me how she's doing?"

The woman tapped on her computer for a few seconds, pulling up Simone's electronic chart, then said, "She's in a hyperbaric chamber right now. Looks like she'll be done in about an hour, and by then visiting hours will have started."

Amelia nodded. That was good. "Does she have carbon monoxide poisoning?" she pressed. She hadn't treated living patients in years, but she knew that was one thing hyperbaric oxygen was used to treat.

"I can't give out that information," the receptionist said, and Amelia didn't blame her. Legally, she had no right to know, even if she really wanted to. The woman pointed to a cluster of chairs, mostly empty at this time of day. "If you want to wait, I'll let you know when she can have visitors."

Amelia nodded. "Thank you."

She headed over to the waiting area, finding an empty chair near the window. She sat for about ten minutes, fidgeting and growing increasingly impatient. Then an older man with graying temples walked into the hospital with a woman his age and told the receptionist, "I'm Simone Olivier's dad. She's here with smoke inhalation and I need to see her."

Amelia got to her feet. She inched closer to Simone's dad while he talked to the receptionist.

"She's receiving a treatment right now so she can't have visitors," the woman explained. "It'll be another forty-five minutes or so."

She explained everything that she'd told Amelia, then invited them to sit down and wait. That was when Amelia stepped in.

"Excuse me, you're Simone's dad?" she asked. "I'm… a coworker."

She'd paused again over her relationship with Simone. She had no idea how often Simone talked to her dad, or what she typically shared with him. Did he know about Amelia? Was there even anything to tell, considering their first date was just twenty-four hours ago?

It felt like something to Amelia, but that didn't mean it was important to the rest of the world.

They shook hands and Simone's father said, "I'm Victor, and this is my wife, Celine."

"Amelia. I'm a doctor—Simone and I met at a scene."

"I figured you didn't work at the firehouse," Victor said. "Celine and I have met Simone's whole crew over the years and I didn't recognize you."

"It's nice that you're so close with her," Amelia said. Her own parents never would have come to the Medical Examiner's Office to meet the people she worked with, but then again, her job involved dead bodies. It wasn't exactly a conducive 'take your parents to work' setting.

"Have you been here long?" Celine asked.

"About ten minutes," Amelia told her. "Do you mind if I wait with you?"

"Of course not," Victor said. "We live about four hours away so we're always grateful to know that Simone has people here looking out for her."

"You must have been on the road pretty early," Amelia said.

Celine nodded. "The ER doctor called us around midnight, after he got her stabilized."

Amelia pointed out that they still had some time to wait before they could see Simone, and offered to go down to the cafeteria and get them all a round of coffee and some breakfast. The Oliviers accepted the coffee offer, and Amelia came back with that plus a bag of breakfast sandwiches in case they changed their mind about the food.

"You don't have to drive up here to see Simone in the hospital often, do you?" she asked upon her return. The question had been nagging at her.

"No, thank God," Celine said.

"She's normally very careful, even if she does have a dangerous job," Victor added.

"She was saving a child," Amelia said. "Maybe that's why she took a risk."

153

She was starting to feel better, and she was even calmer when Simone's doctor came out to give her dad and stepmom an update. He said she was being transported from the chamber to her room and they could all see her in a few minutes. He also said that she'd lost consciousness at the scene, but regained it fairly quickly. She *did* have carbon monoxide poisoning, but it appeared to be mild—the doctor had just been overly cautious by putting her in the hyperbaric chamber.

He also volunteered the fact that the little girl Simone had rescued was also being treated here, and she was in stable condition and expected to make a full recovery.

In short, Simone would be okay, she deserved a medal, and it made Amelia's heart swell with pride and a surprising amount of lust. Of course, she tamped that last emotion down while she sat in the waiting room with Simone's dad and stepmom.

About fifteen minutes later, a nurse appeared and said Simone was ready for visitors. Amelia hung back for a moment, figuring that Simone's parents would want to see her first, but Celine looped her arm in Amelia's and brought her along.

"Anyone who comes to the hospital at the crack of dawn to visit Simone is family in my eyes," she said. "I won't make you wait out there when I'm sure she's dying to see you."

"I'm dying to see her," Amelia confessed.

Simone looked tired and weak, with dark circles under her eyes and an oxygen mask obscuring the lower part of her face. But her eyes contained the same bright, cheerful light they always did. Her dad and Celine both hugged her at the same time, and with her head propped between their shoulders, Simone smiled at Amelia standing near the door.

"Hey, you."

"Hi," Amelia said, waving shyly.

"Come in."

Amelia did. Victor and Celine made room for her at the hospital bed, and Simone grabbed Amelia's hand, pulling her into her arms. "I'm glad you came."

"I was really worried about you," Amelia told her.

"I'm fine, I promise," Simone answered. "I'm sorry I scared all of you."

But she wasn't quite as well as she tried to make everyone think. Saying those few words stole the oxygen from her lungs and sent her into a coughing fit. Soon after, the doctor came in and explained what Simone would need to do once she got released to continue to heal.

It mostly amounted to lots of rest and some antibiotics to prevent infection. The meds wouldn't be a problem, but Amelia couldn't see Simone actually resting like the doctor asked her to. It just didn't seem to be in her nature.

Her parents were under the same impression, because Celine lectured Simone for at least ten minutes after the doctor left. Amelia found it sort of charming—even though they weren't related by blood, it was clear how much Celine cared for Simone.

"We can stay as long as you need us," she said. "We'll take time off work."

"You don't have to do that," Simone objected, her voice froggy. She shot a look to Amelia when they weren't looking, a faint panic in her eyes at the thought of her parents sticking around 'as long as she needed them.'

Amelia smiled. Now that her parents were gone, she'd have done anything for just another day with them. But when she was Simone's age, when it seemed like they would live forever, she would have hated the prospect of her parents practically moving in with her and babying her through an injury.

"I'll be here," she suggested. "You don't have to worry about Simone, Mr. and Mrs. Olivier."

"I'm her father, I'm not sure I can help it," Victor said.

"Are you sure?" Celine asked. "I thought you said you were a doctor... don't you have patients to see?"

"All my patients are dead, so my schedule's flexible," Amelia said, and Celine's mouth dropped open.

"No offense, dear, but are you a *good* doctor?"

Simone started cackling despite her burned lungs. "Celine, she's a medical examiner—like a coroner." Tears sprang to her eyes and she wiped them away, looking to Amelia. "Thank you for that. It's been a rough night and I needed a laugh."

*S*imone ended up getting released around noon. It took forever to get all the paperwork completed and the prescriptions sent to her pharmacy. Amelia volunteered to go out and get lunch for everyone while Simone's parents picked up her meds and drove her home. Then Amelia met them all at Simone's apartment.

It was like night and day compared to Amelia's house —it was in a towering building with many rental units in the heart of downtown. Amelia took the elevator upstairs and found Simone already settling in on the couch, her stepmom arranging pillows around her. Simone's eyes were half-lidded, and it looked like the trip from the hospital had taken it out of her.

"Tired?" Amelia asked.

Simone nodded. "I just need to catch my breath—I'll be okay in a minute."

"You'll take it easy," Celine warned, handing her a bottle of Gatorade they must have picked up at the pharmacy. "Replace your fluids."

Amelia set the takeout bag on the dining table near the door. She'd gotten sub sandwiches and chips for everyone, and she set them all out, then looked around. From the couch, Simone asked, "What do you think? Nothing like your place, is it?"

Simone's apartment was cozy, with hundreds of books and DVDs crammed into the small space. There were lots of throw pillows and Celine had completely cocooned Simone in them, and Amelia noticed pillar candles stacked everywhere.

"It seems very comfortable," Amelia said. "I'm surprised at the number of candles, though, Miss Firefighter."

"You will notice that none of the wicks are burned," Simone said, and indeed, they weren't.

Amelia laughed. "Why do you have them if you don't light them?"

"Some are LED," Simone said, reaching for the one closest to her and flipping a switch at its base. It started to glow and flicker realistically, and she set it back down on the coffee table. "Others I bought because I liked the scent, or just because they make the room feel warm."

"That they do," Amelia agreed, picking up a soft blue one that smelled like crisp linen.

Simone helped herself to her first antibiotic dose, and Celine reminded her that she should eat with her medicine. Amelia passed around the sandwiches, and they all ate and watched reruns of *The Andy Griffith Show,* apparently Victor's favorite show.

Simone fell asleep on the couch for a while, and Amelia alternated between chatting with Celine and Victor and doing what work she could from her phone. After three weeks, they'd finally processed all the bodies and gotten rid of all three refrigerated trucks in the ME office parking lot. There were only a couple of John and Jane Does left in the morgue, but there was still enough paperwork to keep Amelia busy for weeks.

*T*t was getting late when Simone finally woke up again, looking significantly more alert. "What time is it?"

"Five," Victor said. "Are you hungry again?"

"No, I'm fine," Simone said. "It's getting late, though. You two should get on the road if you're going to work tomorrow. I appreciate you coming to take care of me, but I'll be okay."

"You were just in the hospital," Celine argued. "You need someone here with you."

"I'm here," Amelia reminded them. "I'm not going anywhere."

"I don't want you two on the road in the middle of the night," Simone said. "I promise I can take care of myself, and Amelia's a doctor. No offense, but she's far more qualified than you two."

Celine wasn't too happy about leaving, but in the end, Victor pointed out that he was supposed to lead a meeting on Monday morning at work. It took another hour to get them out the door, and by six-fifteen, Simone and Amelia were alone.

Simone let out a long breath and opened her arms for Amelia to curl up next to her. "Come here. I don't know what's more exhausting—carbon monoxide poisoning or having Celine fuss over me all day."

"She's sweet," Amelia said. "So's your dad."

"They are," Simone agreed. "And I appreciate them. But I also appreciate when they leave."

"Yeah, I understand that," Amelia said with a chuckle. She snuggled against Simone, asked her if there was anything she needed, then said, "Oh, I almost forgot —when you were asleep, I got an email from Tom Logan. He got back from Granville and Cal Thomas's paternity test results were waiting for him."

"What's the verdict?"

"Cal Thomas, you *are* the father," Amelia said.

"Does he know yet?" Simone asked. "Oh wow, and do his wife and kid know?"

"I'm not sure," Amelia answered. "The email was pretty brief."

"Well, I'm sure you can squeeze some more info out of Tom in the morning," Simone said. "Want to snuggle and watch a movie with me?"

"That sounds perfect," Amelia said. "What should we watch?"

Simone gestured to her massive DVD collection. "I have pretty much everything. Take your pick."

Amelia got up and perused the shelves while Simone turned on a few more LED candles for mood lighting.

"I've never actually seen *But I'm a Cheerleader*," she said as she popped it into the player. "I hear it's good."

"How did you miss it?" Simone asked skeptically. "It's a gay classic."

"I know... I was in med school when it came out and I barely had time to shower back then, let alone watch movies," Amelia explained.

Simone laughed. "Well, we're going to change that now. Put it in the DVD player."

She reached for the remote and Amelia loaded the disc. She sat on the couch and Simone wrapped her arm around her. With all those candles flickering and Simone's body nestled against her own, Amelia was tempted to say to hell with the movie. She wanted to pounce on Simone and show her just how much she'd worried about her this morning.

But Simone's lungs were damaged, and she needed to take it easy. So Amelia opted for a long, indulgent kiss instead, then settled in and Simone pressed 'play.' As the opening credits rolled, Amelia said, "I'm glad we're changing things. I'm glad you made me find time for love."

"Love?"

Amelia's cheeks flushed. "Yeah. And I'm extra glad that you're okay."

Simone hooked her finger under Amelia's chin and tilted her face up to look into her eyes. "I don't want you to worry about me. I won't leave you."

20

CAL

*C*al hadn't lived aboveground in a month and Elizabeth's sister's house was officially feeling too crowded.

While they waited for their insurance claim to be processed and the reconstruction to begin, Cal and his wife were sleeping in his sister-in-law Trudy's musty basement on a pull-out sofa. Noah had escaped that fate by virtue of his leg injury. He couldn't manage the stairs while he recuperated, so he was staying in the spare bedroom upstairs—though he seemed to have no problem staying out all night with his friends and he'd been keeping up with them just fine, bum leg and all.

So, when he came into the police station on Monday morning to talk to the detective about that dead girl in his stairwell, he was sleep deprived, cranky, and impatient. When they left him alone in what could only be described as an interrogation room for twenty minutes, he got downright angry.

He was tapping his foot and drumming his fingers on the steel table that was the only furniture in the room when the door finally opened and Detective Logan appeared with two cups of coffee and a folder tucked under one elbow.

"Morning, Cal," he said, smiling like he hadn't just given him the run-around. "Thanks for coming in on short notice."

Logan had called last night and asked to meet with him. Cal had no idea what it was about—other than, obviously, the girl he was investigating. Elizabeth had asked Cal at least two dozen times between last night and this morning, "What do you think he wants to talk to you about?"

Just before Cal left the house, he'd snapped, "I told you the first time you asked, I don't know. The answer hasn't changed, damn it."

He felt bad about being cross with her. They were all under stress, living in that little house with her sister. But Elizabeth's nagging had cranked up to level ten ever since the tornado and Cal wasn't sure how much more of it he could take. Hell, a little part of him *hoped* he was in trouble because a night or two in the county jail would probably give him better sleep than he was getting at Trudy's place.

"Sorry to keep you waiting," Logan said as he set one of the coffees down on the table in front of Cal. "Not the greatest cup of joe in the city, but it does the job. You need cream or sugar?"

And risk making this take even longer? "No thanks."

Cal picked up his coffee, and Logan sat down across from him. He took his sweet time, getting comfortable and sipping his coffee. And at last, he said, "Mr. Thomas, are you aware that Megan Hunter was your daughter?"

Cal nearly knocked over his coffee cup. "The dead girl?"

Logan nodded. Then he just sat there, watching Cal's reaction and waiting for him to speak.

"No, she can't be," he said. "Why do you think that?"

"Why do you think she can't be?" Logan countered. "She was nineteen. Your boy is sixteen, right? And you and Elizabeth got married two years before Noah was born. So what were you doing a year before you married Elizabeth?"

"That doesn't matter," he said. "Noah's my only child, and you can ask Elizabeth how hard it was to conceive him. He's our miracle baby."

"Well, the DNA results say otherwise," Logan said, opening the folder and setting a sheet of paper on the table in front of Cal. "This is a paternity test. You ever see one of these before?"

Cal shook his head, and Logan explained what he was looking at—the DNA bands that showed a strong genetic link between Megan Hunter and himself.

"I didn't give you permission to test me," Cal pointed out. "Where did you get my DNA?"

"We have our methods," Logan said. "Did you know that as soon as you discard something in a public trash receptacle, such as a coffee cup, anyone can claim it?"

Cal looked suspiciously at the coffee cup in front of

him now. Clearly they already had what they needed from him, but he pushed it away in any case. He didn't want anything from this deceptive bastard.

"So you're telling me you didn't know Megan Hunter was your daughter," Logan continued. "And you never spoke to her? Never told her where you live?"

"No, I didn't know about her," Cal said. His head was spinning, and all he could think about was how passive-aggressive Elizabeth was going to get when she found out he had a kid with another woman. She wouldn't care that he didn't know about it, or that it had apparently happened before he met her.

"I believe you," Logan said, and Cal felt a morsel of relief. Then Logan pulled another paper out of his folder. This one was thicker and glossy, a photo that looked like it had been printed off someone's social media account. He set it down in front of Cal. "Do you recognize this woman?"

She was middle-aged, with blue eyes and ashy blonde hair, and a few streaks of gray running through it. Cal shrugged, thinking she looked like any other forty-something white woman he knew. "Not particularly."

"What about her name? Nancy Hunter, maiden name Nancy Bridges. That ring any bells?"

Cal shook his head. "Nope. Except I'm assuming she's related to the girl in my basement, given the name."

"That's right, she's Megan's mom," Logan said. "And she remembers you."

Cal just stared at him, waiting for the punchline. Clearly, Detective Logan was waiting for a bigger reaction, some kind of tell, but Cal really didn't have any memory of this woman. "Yeah?"

"I went down to Granville to talk to the Hunters on Saturday," Logan said. "You ever been to Granville?"

"Passed through a few times," Cal said. "So?"

"Do you remember going down there to party when you were younger?" Logan asked. "About twenty years ago?"

It didn't take a rocket scientist to figure out what Logan was driving at. Cal said, "Sure, I probably went down there to party once or twice. Obviously I must have slept with this chick or else we wouldn't be sitting here having this conversation, but I don't remember it. I was twenty. I slept with a lot of chicks."

"You slept with her? Is that all it was?" Logan asked.

Cal's brow furrowed. "I didn't have a relationship with her, if that's what you mean."

"Nancy Hunter didn't describe the encounter nearly so casually," Logan said, sitting back in his chair and folding his arms over his chest.

Christ, what was he driving at now? Did she say she and Cal had been dating or something? He was picturing her sitting in an interrogation room like this one, her husband right next to her, formulating some story about how she and Cal had a whole thing instead of a one-night stand just so her husband wouldn't think she was a slut twenty years ago.

"Look, I don't remember her but I don't deny the possibility of having slept with her," Cal said, trying to get out ahead of the conversation. "Was I a bit of a player in my twenties? Yeah, a lot of guys were. But I never knew she got knocked up. She could have tracked me down and told me but she didn't."

Not that he would have been particularly pleased with that news. Would he have done the right thing, married her instead of Elizabeth? Would his life be completely different now if he had, maybe even better? It was impossible to say.

Detective Logan leaned forward again, looking Cal right in the eyes as he said, "She told me that you date-raped her."

Cal's mouth dropped open. "What? That's ridiculous!"

"She said you got her drunk and took her up to one of the bedrooms in the house you were partying in," Logan went on, "and that she never contacted you about the baby because she didn't want to see her rapist again."

Cal was speechless. Rape! And after twenty years. When he finally managed to gather his thoughts, he said, "Everybody was drunk at that party."

"I thought you didn't remember when you met Nancy," Logan countered.

"I don't, but every party was a drunken one," Cal said. "I never raped anyone."

"That's not what Nancy Hunter says," Logan answered. "She's been carrying that around with her for twenty years, and now her daughter is dead because she was coming here to meet her biological father. And you don't know anything about that?"

"No!" Cal insisted.

"You don't know why your daughter, conceived through rape, would come to your house with a gun?"

Cal was getting antsy on top of the exhaustion, a weird mix. He couldn't think straight and he wanted to get the hell out of there before this escalated any further. "Are you accusing me of something? Or am I free to go?"

Detective Logan sat back in his chair once again. "You're not being charged at this time, Mr. Thomas. But don't leave town."

Cal was out of his seat and heading for the door before the detective had even finished his sentence.

21

SIMONE

*D*espite her best efforts to pretend she was fine, Simone's lungs burned for days after the fire at the apartment building. Every time she inhaled, she was reminded of the smoke that had invaded her cells, turning them crisp and stealing their ability to help her breathe. But two good things came out of that night.

One, she'd saved a little girl. Julie had only minor smoke inhalation and a few small burns where the heat had singed her bare skin, but she was out of the hospital now too and doing just fine.

And the second good thing? She had Amelia all to herself for a few days as she nursed Simone back to health.

They both took a couple days off work and for the first half of the week, Amelia barely left Simone's apartment except to go out a couple of times for food and supplies. She babied Simone even though Simone would have been perfectly capable of taking care of herself if she'd been alone... and Simone exaggerated her helplessness to keep Amelia feeling useful.

They played cards on the couch and worked their way through Simone's DVD collection. They cat-napped —which Simone suspected was as necessary for Amelia as it was for herself. They called Simone's dad once a day for a health progress report, and both he and Celine were as impressed with Amelia as Simone herself was.

By Monday afternoon, Simone was feeling up to a slow, ambling walk around downtown to get some fresh air. They meandered and talked about everything from the mundane—*what's your desert island book?*—to the philosophical—*where do you want to be in ten years?*

And by the time Simone was ready to get back to work on Tuesday, she'd realized something. She was falling in love with Amelia, and where she really wanted to be in ten years was with her.

On Tuesday morning, they went to the diner they'd meant to eat at before Simone's hospitalization. Amelia had to work during the day, and Simone was scheduled to work second shift, so they drove separately but they were both looking for every excuse to spend time together.

"I seem to recall that when we met, you said you didn't date, that you didn't have time for it," Simone teased Amelia over a plate of eggs and hash browns.

"I guess priorities change," Amelia answered, nudging her foot beneath the table.

"Have I thanked you for taking time off work to nurse me back to health?" Simone asked.

"About ten times," Amelia said. "And have I made you promise to be careful if you go out on another fire scene tonight?"

"I'm always careful," Simone said.

"You're still not a hundred percent better," Amelia reminded her.

"Ninety percent is pretty good, though."

Simone was teasing her, but she could see the worry in Amelia's eyes every time they talked about the inevitability of her running into another burning building, giving up her mask for another civilian.

"On a scale of one to ten, how much do you hate my job?" Simone asked.

Amelia took her hand across the table. "I don't *hate* it... I have nothing but respect for what you do and how brave you are. But I never pictured myself dating a firefighter, so it's an adjustment, getting used to worrying about you when you're on the job."

Simone squeezed her hand. "I promise you I'm very good at my job—otherwise I wouldn't have made lieutenant in only five years. I take all the precautions I can. What happened the other day was not an average day in the life of a firefighter."

"But there's always the potential for it to happen again," Amelia pointed out.

"Yes," Simone admitted. "Just like there's the potential for you to catch some kind of crazy bio-terrorist disease during an autopsy, and either of us could get in a car with some crazy rideshare driver and get abducted."

"We both have cars," Amelia pointed out. "Do you even have a rideshare account?"

"Okay, fair enough," Simone said. "Then we could both get hit by a bus as we're leaving this diner."

Amelia laughed. "For the record, the chance of catching any disease, let alone a biological weapon, from a corpse is very low."

"But not zero," Simone insisted.

"Okay, okay," Amelia relented, still laughing. "I get it, life is risky no matter what we do."

"And it's precious," Simone added. "So we have to savor the moments we get with each other."

Their eyes locked, their breakfasts forgotten, and Simone felt the words *I love you* hanging on the tip of her tongue. It was way too soon to say something like that... way too impulsive, and Amelia would probably blame her recent near-death experience for the sudden bout of romanticism. But whether it was fast or not, Simone knew just from looking at Amelia that it was true—she loved this incredible, sexy, beautiful woman.

She was just opening her mouth to say so after all when Amelia's phone started to ring.

She released Simone's hand and broke their gaze. "Sorry, this could be work."

"No problem," Simone said. They had all the time in the world now that they'd found each other. She could tell Amelia how she felt later.

"Hello? ...Yeah, I can be there in about fifteen minutes... Sure thing." Simone listened to Amelia's half of the conversation, and when she hung up, Amelia explained, "That was Tom Logan. He's got Elizabeth Thomas at the precinct and he's about to question her about Megan Hunter. He thinks somebody in that house had to have known she was there and pulled the trigger on that gun."

"Why, though?" Simone asked. "You don't just shoot a stranger for knocking on your door in a tornado."

"She wasn't a stranger, though," Amelia reminded her. "She was Cal Thomas's daughter, and her mom was a rape victim."

Tom had been keeping Amelia in the loop via email for the last few days,

"That gives Megan motivation to shoot Cal, if she tracked him down for that purpose," Simone said. "But how did *she* end up getting shot?"

Amelia shook her head. "I don't know, but hopefully Tom will let us know the answer to that. Anyway, I better get to the office. You sure you're okay to go back to work today?"

Simone leaned across the table and kissed her. "Please stop worrying about me. I'm fine."

In truth, her lungs still burned a little when she exerted herself, but it was nothing she couldn't handle. Besides, she had the rest of the morning to relax before she had to go in for her shift.

"Promise you'll rest?" Amelia asked as they slid out of the booth. It was like she could read Simone's mind.

"Yes," she said. "I am gonna swing by Balch Street on

my way to work and see if I can find that damn hydrant wrench that Williams left there—I keep forgetting about it. But I'll take it easy today and tell the universe not to start any fires tonight. Okay?"

"I hope the universe listens," Amelia said.

22

ELIZABETH

The interrogation room was just as Cal had described it—small, dingy, lonely. Elizabeth had been sitting there for what felt like at least an hour, annoyed because Detective Logan asked her to come in and she did. And then he proceeded to ignore her, probably playing mind games on her while he sat at his desk and ate a donut.

She didn't have to come in. He wasn't charging her with anything, and he hadn't charged Cal when he talked to him the day before. At this point, it sure seemed like the police didn't have any information about that girl and they were just pestering Elizabeth's family.

Making up lies about how Cal had raped the girl's mother.

Digging into ancient history just to threaten Elizabeth's family with a bastard child.

Bogging down the justice system with a case that was clearly an accidental death. Three dozen people had died in Fox County on the day of the tornado—Elizabeth read that in the newspaper. It was tragic, and two of Noah's friends had been among the dead. But why should that Megan girl be any different?

At last, the door opened and Elizabeth sat a little taller as Detective Logan came in. "Sorry to keep you waiting, Mrs. Thomas. Thanks for coming in."

Sorry my foot, she thought.

"Do you know why I wanted to speak with you today?"

"No, and I'd appreciate it if you would just get to the point because I've had a very rough morning already," she said, her voice watery with held-back tears.

"Why is that?" Logan asked, taking a seat across the table from her.

"My husband and I have been fighting a lot lately," she admitted. "I'm sure I don't have to tell you why."

"Humor me," Logan said.

She scowled at him. "Because our house was destroyed, we're living at my sister's place, and my husband has a bastard that you people won't stop hassling us about."

"Had."

"Excuse me?"

"Your husband *had* a bastard. Megan Hunter is dead now." Logan stared fixedly at her, and the affect was unnerving. "Your husband told me that you had trouble conceiving. It must have stung when you found out that he had a child with another woman."

176

"My husband did not rape anyone," Elizabeth snapped. "I don't care what that woman says, she's a liar."

"Rape or not, it was an unplanned pregnancy," Logan said. "It happened after a single encounter, when you and Cal spent *years* trying to conceive Noah."

Elizabeth relaxed just a little bit. "Yes, that knowledge is painful."

"Probably makes you pretty mad too, huh?"

Elizabeth just stared at him, unsure how to answer, her pulse drumming in her ears.

"Mad enough to shoot her?"

"What?!" Elizabeth pushed back from the table. "What are you talking about? I just found out yesterday."

"I don't think that's true," Logan said, slowly shaking his head, his voice even and calm. He leaned forward, his forearms on the steel table. "See, you said yourself that you always lock your doors, so *somebody* had to let Megan Hunter into your house on the morning of the tornado. If it wasn't you, it must have been one of the boys, maybe Noah–"

"Leave Noah out of this," she snapped. "He didn't do anything."

"But did you?" he pressed.

"*No.*"

Detective Logan just sat there, leaning backward in his chair once again, watching her, waiting for her to talk. She was starting to think she might need a lawyer when at last he said, "There's something I didn't tell your husband when he was here yesterday, but I want to tell you. Nancy Hunter—that's Megan's mom—told her daughter that she was date-raped shortly before Megan started college. She wanted her to be careful and avoid a similar fate. She said it was a cautionary tale and she never meant for Megan to figure out that it was actually the story of her conception."

Elizabeth folded her arms, bile rising in her throat, unwilling to look at Logan. "That's awful."

"Yes, what happened to Nancy Hunter *was* awful, and so was what happened to Megan," Logan agreed. "Without hearing that story, she might never have wound up at your door, and she'd probably still be alive today. I don't know how she connected the dots or how she tracked your husband down, but to be perfectly honest, I don't care. All I care about is finding out who shot her."

He paused, and Elizabeth struggled to remain silent. He was clearly waiting for her to confess or else to swear her innocence, but she knew it was a mistake to speak at all. So she pressed her lips together and waited.

"That shot isn't what killed Megan," he said at last. "It was the fall down the stairs, and maybe that was an accident. Maybe the winds from the tornado pushed her in that direction. Maybe whoever let her into the house was just trying to disarm her and they didn't mean to shoot her at all. But I gotta know what happened, and I'll tell you, Elizabeth, there are only so many people that could have gotten into that altercation with Megan."

She stared at the floor, wondering if she and Cal even had the money to hire her a lawyer. The insurance company would eventually reimburse them for all the expenses they'd had to take on since the tornado wrecked their lives, but right now, they were flat broke.

"Elizabeth?" Logan said her name and her eyes involuntarily flicked up to his. "Did you fight with Megan Hunter when she showed up looking for Cal and told you she was his daughter? Was it an accident?"

"No," she said. "I never saw her… until after."

23

AMELIA

*A*melia did an autopsy in the morning—her first non-tornado-related case since the disaster—and checked her email shortly after lunch. She was hoping for word from Tom because she was curious how the Megan Hunter case was going, but he hadn't messaged her.

She figured his talk with Elizabeth Thomas was turning out to be a long one, which probably meant he was getting closer to finding out what happened. So Amelia went about her day, completing a few forms to release bodies to funeral homes. Then around one, she headed to the break room for an afternoon pick-me-up.

She was brewing a fresh pot of coffee when Elise, the office histologist, came in.

"Hey, Dr. Trace," she said as she headed for the fridge. "How's your girlfriend doing?"

Amelia's cheeks colored. She'd called in on Monday morning and asked Reese to let everyone know she wouldn't be in for a day or two, depending on how long it took Simone to feel better. A little part of her knew, even while she was on the phone, that it was a bad idea to give the office gossip that much ammunition. And here it was a little more than twenty-four hours later and the whole office seemed to know she had a girlfriend before she and Simone had even defined their relationship.

She just had to laugh. She knew this would happen, so had some subconscious part of herself told Reese about Simone's smoke inhalation on purpose? Amelia had to admit, 'girlfriend' had a nice ring to it.

"She's doing much better," Amelia said, not bothering to correct Elise's terminology. That *was* the direction she and Simone were headed in, wasn't it? "I am still worried about her going to work tonight, though."

"Understandable," Elise said. "I wouldn't want my girlfriend running into burning buildings... if I had one."

"How was everything here yesterday without me?" Amelia asked. Things were returning to normal, but she still felt guilty taking time off while the mass disaster protocol was still technically in place and the workloads were still so heavy.

"We survived," Elise said, pulling a container of yogurt out of the fridge and then fishing for a spoon in one of the drawers. "There was a little mishap with my tissue samples. Honestly, I'm surprised we haven't goofed up before that, what with how busy we've been."

"What was the goof?" Amelia asked.

"Oh, don't worry, I caught it pretty quickly," Elise said. "One of the autopsy assistants switched the labels for two different decedents before they delivered the tissue samples to me."

"That could definitely be a huge problem," Amelia said. "How did you figure it out?"

"Luckily they had different blood types," Elise said. "And you know me—I've got an eye for detail. Once I noticed the blood types weren't right, I figured out the problem and got it all sorted out."

"We're lucky to have you," Amelia said. "Thanks for catching that."

"It's my job," Elise said with a humble shrug.

She went over to the long table in the room to eat her yogurt, and Amelia mused over how messy those cases could have gotten if Elise hadn't found that mistake. She was staring at the coffee pot, listening to it percolate, when Noah Thomas and his blood transfusion popped into her head.

Tom had said he was a universal recipient—AB+. And hadn't Cal Thomas said he wanted to donate blood for his son because he was a universal donor?

No way...

Amelia rushed out of the breakroom, with Elise calling behind her, "Don't you want your coffee?"

Back in her office, Amelia did a quick search on blood group inheritance. It had been a while since she needed this information, but she faintly remembered something from medical school about the various phenotypes, with dominant and recessive alleles...

Yes, there. She found the answer she was looking for.

There wasn't a lot you could rule out if you didn't

know the mother's blood type, and as far as Amelia was aware it hadn't come up in the course of this case. But one thing you definitely *could* rule out was a Type O father with a Type AB child. It just wasn't possible.

Amelia switched over to her email and found the message where Tom had told her that Cal was Megan's biological father. He'd included the lab report as an attachment, and Amelia checked it to be sure. Right there at the top of the page: Cal Thomas, O negative.

He might not have known that he had a kid in Granville for the last nineteen years, but did he know the boy he was raising *wasn't* his child?

She picked up her desk phone and dialed Tom's number. It rang a few times and went to voicemail. Amelia knew he was talking to Elizabeth today, and there was no way he'd want to cut her lose without asking her about Noah's paternity.

Amelia called the main police switchboard. When a dispatcher picked up, she identified herself and said, "I'm looking for Detective Tom Logan. I believe he's interviewing someone right now."

"Do you want to leave a message?" the dispatcher asked, chomping on gum.

"No, it's urgent," Amelia said. "Can you send someone into the room?"

"Sure, what would you like them to say?"

"Ask them to tell Tom that Cal Thomas can't be Noah's father because–"

"Hold on, hold on," the gum chewer said, "I can't write that fast."

Amelia let out a huff, trying not to make her frustration apparent over the phone. "You know what? Scratch that. I'm only a few minutes away, so just tell Tom not to let Elizabeth go until I get there. Okay?"

"...not to let Elizabeth go..." Amelia gritted her teeth, and when she was sure that the dispatcher had her message right, she hung up. This would be easier and faster to explain in person, and anyway, she was sort of curious to see the woman's reaction when Tom told her what she'd just discovered.

There was very little chance she didn't know that Cal wasn't Noah's father, unless she'd been sleeping with multiple men at the time of conception, and yet she hadn't seen fit to bring it up to the police, even after they'd uncovered Megan's relation to Cal. But what was the motivation for hiding it?

*A*bout ten minutes later, Amelia had a police precinct visitor's badge pinned to her shirt and she was being led through the halls to the interrogation rooms. The officer who was escorting her knocked on one of the doors, and a moment later, Tom poked his head out.

"Dr. Trace, thanks for coming," he said, then looked back into the room. "Mrs. Thomas, I need to step out for a minute. Do you need anything? Coffee, water, bathroom break?"

"I need to not spend all day here," she said, her tone sharp.

Tom ignored her comment and stepped into the hall, closing the door behind himself. The other officer headed back to the front of the precinct, and Amelia conveyed what she'd figured out.

"So, does that help you?" she asked, somewhat doubtful, when she'd finished catching him up to speed. To her, it seemed like just another complication in an already difficult case, but maybe it would mean something to Tom.

"It definitely doesn't hurt," he said, "although you kind of lost me with the science talk. You want to come in and observe, help me out if I need more official terminology?"

"I doubt she'll ask you for the definition of an allele, but I was hoping I'd get to watch," Amelia confessed.

Tom opened the door, holding it for her as they both stepped back into the room. He introduced Amelia, and Elizabeth said she remembered her from the day of the tornado. Amelia and Tom sat down beside each other on the opposite side of the table from where Elizabeth sat, and Tom folded his hands on top of it.

"Dr. Trace just told me something pretty interesting," he said. He paused for effect so long that even Amelia was tempted to fill the silence, then he asked, "How many people know that Cal is not Noah's father?"

"What?" Elizabeth's mouth dropped open. "Yes, he is."

"Not biologically," Tom said. "Tell her the stuff about the As and Bs and alleles, Dr. Trace."

Amelia repeated it all again, putting it into layman's terms as much as possible. While she talked, Tom studied Elizabeth's reaction. Then he asked, "So, how many people know?"

Elizabeth folded her arms over her chest defensively. "I don't see how this is relevant to Megan Hunter."

"Let me be the judge of that," Tom replied. "Give me a number, Mrs. Thomas."

She rolled her eyes. "As few as I could manage." Then the dam broke and she started being more forthcoming, meeting Tom's gaze again. "I never wanted Noah to feel like he was different from the other kids. It's so easy to get a chip on your shoulder when you're growing up, I didn't want him to think his dad wasn't his dad."

"Sounds like you've been holding onto that for a lot of years," Tom said. He was being sympathetic, making Elizabeth open up to him, and it seemed to be working.

"I couldn't tell anyone—not even Cal," she said. "I was too afraid that Noah would find out if *anyone* knew."

Tom leaned forward, gave her a sad smile and asked softly, "Did you have an affair, Elizabeth?"

"What? No!" She was angry again in a split second, offended at the mere suggestion. "I am not a cheater!"

"But you were desperate to have a child," Tom countered. "How did you get pregnant?"

She crossed her arms over her chest. "Don't you think that's a personal question?"

He leaned back, mirroring her posture. "If you don't

want to talk about that, I could tell you what I think happened to Megan Hunter on the morning of the tornado. Because I'll tell you right now, I'm not buying the fact that you didn't see her until after she was dead."

Elizabeth's lips went thin and tight and she practically spat her answer. "I went to a fertility clinic."

"Without Cal?"

"I already told you, I didn't want anyone to know, for Noah's sake," she said. "Besides, the longer we tried to get pregnant without any luck, the worse Cal felt about himself. He never said it in so many words, but I think he felt emasculated. He... you're not going to repeat any of this to him, are you?"

"The paternity, or the part about his manhood?" Tom asked with a smirk.

Elizabeth frowned. "After a while, he couldn't... finish. Because he was embarrassed. And we were never going to have a baby that way. I figured it would be better for both of us if I helped the process along, so I got tested. The doctor told me I was fertile, so it was likely that Cal wasn't. After all the trouble we'd already had I knew telling him his little swimmers weren't swimming wasn't going to help, so... I found an anonymous donor and I got inseminated."

"And told Cal it was his child."

"Yes! Does that make me the worst person in the world?" she asked, in a tone that made it clear she wasn't really asking. "All I wanted was a family, and I did what was necessary to get it."

"And when your husband's daughter—his biological

daughter—showed up unannounced with a gun in her hand, accusing your husband of raping–"

"Stop saying that!" Elizabeth cried.

"*Raping* her mother," Tom went on, "I think you lost your shit. I think you were looking at proof that your husband gave another woman something he wouldn't or couldn't give you, and you shot Megan."

"*No*," Elizabeth said, "*that's not what happened!*"

"Tell me what *did* happen."

"I never saw her," she insisted. "I've already told you on several occasions, Cal had already left for work and I was in the kitchen drinking my morning coffee when the tornado siren went off. It hit quickly. I barely had time to get to the basement and luckily the boys were already down there. *I never saw that girl.*"

"So she never knocked on the door, and you didn't answer it?" Tom asked. Elizabeth shook her head. "She didn't tell you who she was and there wasn't an altercation as a result?"

"*No.*"

"You're telling me that a girl died in your house and you had no idea she was there, you never heard the gun go off? She had a bullet wound in her arm and the autopsy confirmed it was a perimortem injury. That means it occurred very close to the time of death."

"It... it was very loud," Elizabeth said. "Between the winds and the siren, and the boys yelling because they were scared... I never saw her and I didn't hear a gunshot."

Tom sighed. "That's bullshit, Elizabeth. Unless...

Noah or one of his friends shot Megan? Are you covering for one of them?"

"They weren't involved!" she said.

"But you were," Tom insisted. "Tell me what happened or I'll have no choice but to assume that you're covering for something Noah did."

"Fine!" Elizabeth hissed. "I opened the door!"

Amelia was holding her breath. Tom sat calmly beside her, his demeanor completely unchanged even though he'd finally gotten what he wanted.

"She told me she was looking for Cal," Elizabeth said. "I said he wasn't home and she didn't believe me. She came into my house and she told me... what her mom said he did."

She was clearly struggling with the idea that her husband was capable of such an awful act—she couldn't even name it.

"She took out the gun and said she wasn't leaving until she got to talk to him," Elizabeth said.

"What did she want to talk to him about?" Tom asked.

"She wanted to confront him," Elizabeth answered. "She wanted to tell him what it felt to be the result of... *rape.*" She whispered the word this time. "She wanted to know why he did it. I told her she had the wrong guy, the wrong house. And then she turned toward the basement."

"Where Noah was," Tom supplied.

"Yes," Elizabeth confirmed. "I couldn't let her go down there. I couldn't let her tell him what his dad did.

189

So I reached for the gun. We fought. I wasn't trying to shoot her, I just wanted her to leave. The gun went off by accident, and for a second I thought the whole damn world was ending because the tornado siren started ringing at the same time."

She buried her face in her hands and in a moment of compassion, Tom pulled a travel pack of tissues out of his pocket, sliding them across the table to her. She took one, then continued.

"The kitchen door blew open," she said. "It must not have latched all the way when the girl came inside. The winds were so strong. I swear I didn't push her. I was watching the blood trickle down her arm from the gunshot—we were both kinda spooked by that—and then all of a sudden this big gust blew through and it was like she disappeared. Took me a few seconds to realize she fell, and then all I could think was that I needed to get the hell down to the basement too or the tornado was going to suck me up."

She took a long, ragged breath and looked at Tom again. "I was angry at Cal, and at her for showing up at my house. But I never wanted to hurt her... you have to believe me."

"Where is the gun now, Elizabeth?" Tom asked.

She opened her mouth, then paused. Her brow furrowed, and she shook her head. "I don't know. You didn't find it in the house?"

"No," Tom said. "Are you sure you didn't stash it somewhere, Elizabeth?" When she didn't answer, he relaxed into his seat, explaining, "I understand that you didn't mean to hurt her, but the fact of the matter is, Megan Hunter is dead. A nineteen-year-old who had her whole life ahead of her. Dead because of what your husband did to her mother twenty years ago, and what you did to her when she showed up at your house. Things will go a lot better for you from here on out if you just tell me the whole truth, and cooperate."

Elizabeth covered her mouth with the tissue, seeming to consider her options. And then she said, "I think I better have a lawyer now. And I get a phone call, right?"

24

ELIZABETH

*D*etective Logan let Elizabeth sit in the interrogation room for at least another thirty minutes. It seemed to be one of his favorite ways to make her uncomfortable—promising he'd be right back, then disappearing for long stretches.

Well, it gave her lots of time to think about the fact that she'd just confessed to shooting Megan Hunter... whether it had been intentional or not. She also thought about how it should have been Cal in this situation. She was his daughter, and she was mad at him, not Elizabeth.

She also thought a lot about Noah. Would he find out everything now? It seemed unlikely that Elizabeth would get out of all this without at least a trial at this point, and if there was a trial, everything would come out. Sixteen years of protecting him from this ugly truth and it had all fallen apart in the time it took for a tornado to sweep through their neighborhood and destroy their home.

Their family.

Now Noah had a rapist for a father and a murderer for a mother. Or a manslaughterer, if she was lucky with the charges.

At last, the door to the interrogation room opened again and a different police officer, one she didn't recognize, came in. "Elizabeth? I'm going to take you to a phone so you can make a call, and then I'll book you into a holding cell for the night, okay?"

Her heart jumped into her throat. This was really happening to her.

"And then what?" she asked.

"You'll be held overnight, and in the morning you'll have a chance to meet with your lawyer, or a public defender if you need one. Then you'll go to court to be arraigned."

"What am I being charged with?" she asked, the words coming out as a squeak.

"Voluntary manslaughter," he said, and she wasn't sure whether to be relieved or not.

He gestured for her to stand, and she followed him out of the room and down the hall. They passed a bunch of cubicles where officers in uniform typed up case reports and ran background checks and whatever else cops did at their desks. Elizabeth's mind was reeling and she was too busy trying to figure out if she knew any lawyers to pay them much attention.

But she thought she heard Detective Logan's voice somewhere in those cubicles, and her ears automatically honed in on him.

"–really wish we had that gun," he was saying. "I

mean, we've got a confession but without physical evidence, you know how shaky that is..."

And then the officer opened a door and guided Elizabeth into another room, and Logan's voice faded out. Was he talking about her case? Her apparently shaky case? It was a tiny morsel of hope but she clung to it.

"The phone is there," the officer said, pointing to a desk with an old-fashioned black phone on it. "If you need to look up a phone number, I can help you with that."

"No, I've got it memorized," she said, sitting down.

"I'll be right outside," the officer said. "Come out when you're done."

She nodded and waited until the door had shut completely behind him before she picked up the receiver. It was a miracle her brain was working at all in the state she was in, but she managed to dial Cal's cell, probably from muscle memory more than anything else.

When he answered, Elizabeth couldn't decide if she felt more angry or guilty. "Cal, I've been arrested."

"Oh, so now you're speaking to me," he said gruffly. It was true, she'd been giving him the silent treatment since the day before, when she found out he was that girl's father. Now was no time for pettiness, though—not when she was facing a whole night in this cinderblock-walled hell hole.

"Cal, did you hear me? I'm calling you from the police station!"

There was a pause on his end of the line as he

digested that information, then he asked, "Arrested for what?"

She could barely say the words: "I shot that girl."

There was silence on the other end of the line while Cal processed that. Maybe hated her? That girl was his daughter, after all. His daughter that he'd conceived with some strange woman, and yet he couldn't give Elizabeth the son she'd so desperately wanted.

Once the flood gates opened, she couldn't stop talking. "It was an accident, but they're charging me with voluntary manslaughter," she told him. "I have to go to court in the morning and that detective that keeps pestering us, he said they need the gun or else their case is weak. I need you to get me a lawyer, Cal–"

"With what money, Elizabeth?" he asked. It was the same thing she'd been thinking earlier, but God help her if she had to rely on a public defender to get her out of this mess. When had her life turned into a *Jerry Springer* episode?

"And I need something else," she went on, shooting a cautionary glance toward the door, the police officer standing guard right outside. She could see his shoulder in the reinforced window, and she knew someone would listen to this call, but at least no one was watching her.

And at least Cal didn't know about Noah yet. It would come out during the trial, Elizabeth was sure of it. But for now, she desperately needed him to be on her side. Even if she was still furious with him for having a baby with that other woman.

"Cal, please help me," she begged.

"Okay," he said with a sigh. "I'm listening."

Things had been tense between them for the last few weeks, ever since the tornado. Elizabeth knew Cal didn't like relying on other people, and he wasn't her sister's number one fan either. But he wasn't what Detective Logan said he was—he couldn't have done what he said Cal did to that woman. And he always came through for Elizabeth when she needed him.

She thought for a moment. How was she going to ask for what she needed without immediately alerting the police?

"Since I'm stuck in here, there's something I need you to take care of. I told the insurance assessor I'd go out to the house this afternoon to take pictures, but clearly I can't go," she said, speaking slowly and praying Cal would get her drift.

"When did you talk to the assessor? I've been dealing with the insurance."

"Cal, it's important to get those *pictures* this afternoon," she said. "And I need you to pay special attention to the fireplace. The surround is an antique and I'd like to know if there's anything *inside the fireplace* that we can salvage."

"Babe, the whole house is rubble," Cal said. "I know you like that cast iron surround, but it's not safe to go down there. Besides, that surround is probably totaled like everything else."

Oh Lord... Cal never was good at charades, but Elizabeth couldn't stop thinking about what she overheard Detective Logan saying about the gun that girl brought into her house. The cops needed it—he'd mentioned it twice, once in the interrogation room and once in the bullpen.

If Elizabeth wanted to get out of here, that gun needed to disappear for good. It was already a miracle that the house had been in such shambles that the police hadn't been able to find it on their initial search of the property. And now she was relying on her worthless husband to not only pick up on her hints, but also to follow through.

Lord help me.

"Cal," she tried again, "The police are *gunning* for me and I'm going to be in jail all night. I need you to go to the house for me."

"Elizabeth, I've *been* the one dealing with…" He trailed off and she held her breath, hoping he'd finally connected the dots.

She really couldn't speak in any more explicit terms than she already had, and even then, she was pushing it. But there was one more thing she had to say. "I love you, Cal. I never meant for any of this to happen, but it was all for our family. When you see Noah, hug him for me, okay? I know he's sixteen and he thinks he's too old for that, but do it anyway, please. He's our miracle baby, after all."

Especially considering she'd spent the last sixteen years thinking that Cal was sterile. But now was no time to get bitter.

She ended the call and knocked on the door, and the police officer led her down another hall to a row of holding cells. Each one had a hard steel bench, a toilet in one corner, and absolutely no privacy. If there was anything to be grateful for, it was that, at least for the moment, they were all empty.

He opened the door to the first cell and Elizabeth went inside. She jumped when the door rolled shut behind her, and her heart climbed into her throat. She sat down on the bench and tried to control her breathing—tried not to think of the fact that this would be her life for God knew how long if Cal hadn't understood what she was trying to tell him on the phone.

Or if he understood, but chose not to help her.

What if he found out about Noah before he did this one last thing for her?

She closed her eyes and breathed deep, the air filling her lungs in jagged inhales. She was here because she wanted the best life possible for her son. She was here because her husband raped some poor woman and his bastard daughter had showed up on their doorstep, wanting to know what kind of monster she'd come from.

*T*hirty minutes later, Cal was climbing through the rubble of his ruined home with his cell phone out, pretending to take insurance pictures just in case anyone asked what he was doing. Not that the story would have held much water—the insurance assessor had taken his own pictures weeks ago.

The journey down into the basement was precarious, with sharp splinters of wood sticking up all over the place, ready to impale Cal if he tripped. Not to mention all the nails and other bits of rusty metal waiting to give him tetanus. And Cal didn't even know if he'd understood Elizabeth correctly. He thought she wanted him to come down here and find the gun in the fireplace, but wasn't that one of the first places the cops would have looked for it?

And why, exactly, was he sticking his neck out for her? He slept with some college chick twenty years ago and had a baby he didn't even know about, and for that, his wife had been furious with him, giving him the silent treatment ever since he got home from the precinct last night.

But he'd told her about the rape allegation and she hadn't hesitated to take his side. Elizabeth believed him when he said they'd both been drunk, and consent was a whole different animal back then. Right or wrong, she was on his side. She was his wife. And he owed it to her to at least try to find this gun.

Besides, how was he going to raise a teenager with her behind bars?

The only luck he'd had all day was the fact that the chimney had remained relatively untouched during the tornado, and there wasn't a ton of debris stacked up in front of the fireplace. He'd been bracing himself to come out here and find the house completely impassable. But in reality, it was slow going but relatively easy to navigate.

He crouched down and shuffled a few broken boards and crumbling bricks aside, then reached into the back of the fireplace. It was pitch-black inside, and all he could see was ashes.

"Damn it, Elizabeth," he grumbled as he stuck his hand inside.

There was nothing inside the flue, or on the smoke shelf where he'd guessed she'd hidden the gun. He climbed all the way onto the hearth and moved aside the grate at the very back of the fireplace, then probed his hand inside the ash pit beneath the hearth.

The ash was cool and oddly fluffy, and he had to reach in a few inches past his wrist before his fingertips touched metal. He closed his hand around the butt of the gun and as soon as he'd pulled it out he cursed himself for using his bare hand. Now the fucking thing had his prints on it as well as his wife's.

For a split second, he wondered if *that* was what she was after all along. What if she didn't want him to dispose of the gun for her? What if she wanted him to incriminate himself? She *was* more pissed at him over the girl than she'd ever been in their marriage. And he'd just gone along with her plan like an idiot.

Well, what's done is done, he thought, shaking ash from the gun and sticking it in the pocket of his sweatshirt. If his prints were on it, that was all the more motivation to get rid of it.

Cal started the arduous process of climbing back out of the rubble. He made it halfway up what remained of the stairs when he heard the creaking noise of footsteps over loose floorboards. The whole damn house was loose boards now, but he was pretty sure the sound was coming from what remained of the ground floor, right in his path.

Fuck, what now?

He froze on the stairs, wondering if the police had decoded his phone conversation with Elizabeth already and were here to arrest him as an accomplice.

Cal wasn't cut out for life in prison, and he hated the idea of Noah being stuck with Trudy if both his parents were incarcerated. He stayed still and listened hard as the floorboards creaked overhead. Then he noticed a shaft of light coming through the floor and realized he could see into the kitchen.

There was only one of them, not a whole SWAT team. And it was a petite-looking woman.

Cal's pulse was racing and his fight-or-flight instinct kicked in. He chose flight, deciding to bum-rush her and get the hell out of here. If he moved fast enough and blindsided her, she wouldn't get a good look at him and she wouldn't be able to identify him. No one would ever have to know he was here.

He took the gun out of his pocket just in case. He'd never fired one before and he didn't even know how to check if the safety was off, but he felt a little more confident with his plan once it was in his palm.

He broke into a sprint, running up the basement stairs, but the minute he stepped around the corner, the woman screamed and he froze again, raising the gun instinctively.

She was a blonde in plainclothes, and her eyes were wide with terror. She cried, "Please, don't shoot!"

SIMONE

*S*imone was crouched behind a trash can at the curb when she heard Amelia's voice, high and wavering, begging for her life. It sent an electric jolt through Simone's spine, and flooded her veins with adrenaline. Suddenly she was hyper focused, alert, tensed to act just like she always felt right before she ran into a burning building.

Someone needed her help, and this time, it was the woman she loved.

Simone tightened her grip on the hydrant wrench in her hand. She'd come to retrieve it before work, just like she'd planned, only when she got here, she recognized Cal Thomas's car parked on the sidewalk. That alone wouldn't have been unusual—this was his neighborhood, after all. But he'd parked it way down the street, not near his house at all, and it had given Simone a bad feeling in her gut.

So she'd retrieved the wrench and then found a

vantage point from which she could observe and figure out what Cal was up to. He'd been in the house—what was left of it—for about five minutes when Simone heard Amelia scream and her blood ran icy in her veins.

She hadn't noticed Amelia arriving, and she definitely wouldn't have allowed her to go into that house if she'd seen her. What the hell was she doing here?

Simone ran as quietly as she could across the lawn, then crept around one wall of the house—one of only two still standing. She paused at a window with spider-webbed glass, probably cracked from the pressure and movement when the rest of the house came down. It provided decent cover, making it difficult for someone on the inside of the house to see her.

Simone crouched low and peeked into the kitchen. The first thing she saw was Amelia standing stock still in the doorway, her hands up defensively.

The next thing she noticed was Cal Thomas standing about ten feet from Amelia in the basement doorway, pointing a gun at her. Cal looked nervous, and clearly Amelia was too.

The neighborhood was pretty quiet at this hour—it was still early afternoon, so most people were at work, and the Thomas house was surrounded on two sides by other houses that had been decimated by the tornado. That meant there were no immediate neighbors to get help from, and Simone would never forgive herself if something happened to Amelia while she sat around, twiddling her thumbs and waiting for the police to arrive. She was going to have to get her out of there herself.

Simone turned and crept as quickly and silently as she could back around the corner of the house. On the way, she tried to formulate a plan, but her mind was a blank but for one repeating mantra: *save Amelia.*

She reached the edge of the wall, what should have been the corner of the house if the rest of it was still standing. She was at Cal's back, just a few steps away from the kitchen door that Megan Hunter must have come through on the day she died.

As soon as Simone stepped out from behind the wall, Amelia would see her behind Cal and that might give her away. So Simone had to be ready to act.

She looked down at the hydrant wrench in her hand. It was about a foot and a half long, heavy, with a brass spanner head at one end that could do some serious damage. The idea of hitting Cal Thomas with it made Simone's stomach turn, but he had a gun pointed at Amelia. Given a choice between her and anyone else in the world, Simone wouldn't hesitate to save Amelia.

Tightening her grip, she stepped around the wall. Amelia's eyes immediately went to her, and Cal whirled around. Simone brought the wrench down as hard as she could across his wrist, hoping to knock the gun from his hand.

It fired. Amelia screamed, and so did Cal. Simone's heart was pounding so hard she could feel it against her rib cage.

Cal was on his knees, cradling one hand to his chest, the gun lying on the floor. Simone kicked it away as Amelia rushed over to her. Apparently, doctor mode had kicked in for her just like firefighter mode had kicked in for Simone a few minutes ago, because she was asking, "Is everyone okay? Anyone shot?"

"I'm fine," Simone said. "Are you?"

"I'm okay," Amelia answered.

"She broke my fucking wrist!" Cal bawled.

"That's what you get for pointing guns at people," Simone said, grabbing Amelia's hand. "Come on, we all need to get out of here—this house isn't safe."

Cal wasn't moving, far too absorbed in his pain, so she hooked a hand under his arm.

"Come on, it's not your legs that are broken," she said, urging him to stand.

"Where's the gun?" Amelia asked.

"I kicked it away," Simone said. "I think it fell down the stairs."

"I wasn't really going to shoot you, I swear," Cal told Amelia, still cradling his hand. He told Simone, "You didn't have to hit me."

"That's not how I saw it at the time," Simone answered gruffly. "Come on."

With Amelia's help, Simone got Cal to his feet and the three of them made it out to the lawn, a safe distance away in case that bullet hit something structural and caused the house to collapse further. They sat Cal down on the curb, and just as Simone was reaching for her phone to call him an ambulance, she noticed red police flashers at the far end of the street.

"Who called the cops?" Simone asked.

"I did," Amelia said. "Tom got a confession out of

Elizabeth Thomas this afternoon, and he mentioned the fact that nobody ever recovered the gun. I knew you were coming here to look for your wrench, and I just got a really bad feeling that something was going to happen. I tried to call you, but you didn't pick up so I just came."

"Told you this neighborhood has shit reception," Cal said.

"Quiet," Simone warned him. He was ruining the moment. She turned back to Amelia. "You came to rescue me?"

Amelia nodded. "And you ended up rescuing me."

"I told you, I wasn't gonna shoot you," Cal interrupted.

"You can tell that to the police," Simone told him.

The one responding to the scene turned out to be none other than Tom Logan in his unmarked SUV, an emergency bubble light flashing on his dashboard. He hopped out of the vehicle, seeming a little more spry than he had just a month ago, and asked, "Everybody okay?"

"We're fine," Amelia answered. "You knew that Mrs. Thomas was going to tell her husband where the gun was, didn't you?"

"I was hoping," Tom admitted. "Didn't expect you to go all vigilante and come out here by yourself, though."

Amelia turned to Simone with a smile. "I had to save my girlfriend."

Simone beamed. "I like the sound of that."

They took turns explaining what happened to Tom, and Simone told him where the gun was. He asked her to get her crew out here to safely retrieve it, then he told

Cal, "Stand up and turn around. You're under arrest for evidence tampering and assault with a deadly weapon."

"I wasn't going to shoot her!" Cal shouted, but Tom just grabbed him by the shoulders of his shirt and hauled him to his feet.

"Turn around," he repeated.

Cal screamed as soon as Tom touched his wrist with a handcuff, and Simone figured it really was broken. She'd hit him as hard as she could, knowing she was only going to get one opportunity to catch him off guard. Whether he'd planned to shoot Amelia or not, Simone didn't regret playing it safe.

"Dr. Trace, will you go to my trunk and get the first aid kit there?" Tom asked. "There's an inflatable splint in it."

She did as he asked, jogging over while Tom Mirandized Cal, and coming back with something that looked like a clear plastic water wing for in the pool. She helped Tom slide it over Cal's wrist and inflate it, stabilizing his injury. Then Tom got creative with the cuffs, securing both hands behind Cal's back.

"Let's go," he said, guiding Cal toward the car. "If you're lucky, you'll get booked into the cell right next to your wife."

He stuffed Cal into the back of his SUV, then drove off the way he'd come. Simone would need to call the firehouse and ask a couple of the more experienced guys to come out and retrieve the gun. But first, she wanted a moment alone with Amelia.

She took both her hands, kissing her knuckles before

wrapping her arms around Amelia's waist. "I was so scared when I heard you scream. I thought I was going to lose you."

"*I* was scared when I realized what Tom was up to," Amelia said. "I kept picturing you out here looking for your wrench, and Mr. Thomas with that gun..."

"I love you," Simone said.

Amelia met her gaze. "You do?"

"Yes, with my whole heart," Simone told her. "I know it's fast, but I also know it's the real deal. I want to be with you, Amelia, even if we're both busy as hell and we only ever get to see each other a few times a week—or even a few times a month. I want any amount of time that I can get with you, and I promise, I'll do my best not to make you worry."

Amelia smiled, and smacked Simone's shoulder. "You're not doing a very good job of it lately."

"I'm sorry. I'll work on it."

"You better," Amelia said. "Because I love you too."

27

AMELIA

*W*hile Simone's crew worked together to find the gun, Amelia and Simone stood on the lawn and watched. After a while, Simone put her head on Amelia's shoulder and groaned.

"I can't believe I still have to go work a shift after this," she said, her words muffled against Amelia's shirt. Then she lifted her head and whispered, her breath hot against Amelia's ear, "All I really want to do is drag you to bed and show you how damn much I love you."

"I want that too," Amelia said, her hand sliding surreptitiously down to cup Simone's butt. She gave it a little squeeze, then brought her hand back up to Simone's waist. "What time do you get off?"

"Five a.m."

"And I don't need to be at work again until eight," Amelia said. "So here's what we're going to do: you're going to come over to my place after your shift, and we're going to make love, maybe have breakfast—we'll see how much we can do with three hours."

"More like two, once you account for both of our commutes," Simone pouted. "I just want to quit my job and run away with you."

Amelia grinned. "That *does* sound nice, but I'm pretty sure you'd regret that. Didn't you say yourself that you were never going to let a woman get in the way of your career?"

"That was before I fell in love with you," Simone said. "But you're right—I guess we need to keep earning money so we can afford to run away together someday, when we're both retired."

Amelia stole a quick kiss. "Come see me in the morning. I'll make it worth your while."

"It always is."

*A*t five-thirty the next morning, Amelia was waiting for Simone. She'd gotten up two hours before her alarm typically went off and put on a pot of coffee. Then she'd hopped in the shower and got squeaky clean before dressing in a silky negligee— something more conducive to going back to bed than going to work. And that was exactly what she had in mind.

When Simone arrived, Amelia grabbed her by the collar of her station uniform and pulled her into the house. "How are your lungs this morning?"

"Healing," Simone told her, "but they also think you're insanely hot in this little nightie and they want me to fuck your brains out."

She was running her fingers along the bottom hem, brushing her fingertips over the front of Amelia's thigh and then trailing between her legs. Heat bloomed in Amelia's core and she pulled Simone further into the living room.

"I made coffee," she said. "And there's more croissants. I figured we could make breakfast sandwiches–"

"Or I could just eat you instead," Simone answered, nipping at Amelia's lower lip.

"Yeah," Amelia breathed, "that was plan B."

"I like plan B," Simone said. She walked Amelia backward toward the couch, asking, "Here okay?"

Amelia nodded and Simone dropped to her knees. She buried her face in the silky material, kissing Amelia's swollen clit through the fabric. She had her hands on Amelia's hips, bracing her and holding her in place, and when she bowed down and nudged her way beneath the negligee, she let out a pleased hum as she discovered that Amelia wore nothing beneath it.

Amelia closed her eyes and savored the sensation of Simone's tongue on her clit, and gliding up and down her already slick pussy. She spread her feet a little wider and gasped when Simone licked deep in her folds.

"I was going to make you take it easy," Amelia told her. "I had every intention of tying your wrists to my bedpost if that's what it took to make you rest while I took care of you."

Simone pushed two fingers into Amelia's slit and her thighs shook as a wave of pleasure rippled through her. "I'd let you tie me to your bed," she said as her fingers slowly worked in and out of her. "In fact, I love that idea. But only if you let me tie you up another time."

Was that a challenge?

It was a damn hard one, considering how turned on Amelia already was. She wanted nothing more than to grab onto the back of Simone's head and press her face between her legs until she came against Simone's mouth. Maybe they could do one, then the other? They had a few hours...

Simone brought her thumb up to Amelia's clit, her fingers still massaging her core. Her other hand snaked up beneath Amelia's negligee and grabbed her breast, kneading and toying with her nipple. And the mix of sensations was too much. Amelia was too close to the edge.

"Oh God," she gasped, taking Simone's head in both her hands. "Fuck me. Put your mouth on me. Please."

She guided Simone's tongue where she wanted it, then braced herself on the back of the couch as Simone's wet tongue lapped increasingly frantic circles around her clit. Simone's fingers pumped inside her, and Amelia moved her hips against Simone's mouth, desperate for release.

"I'm close," she whined, "I'm so close, baby. I love you."

"I love you too," Simone answered, her words muffled as she said them with her lips pressed to Amelia's most sensitive area. She thrust her fingers deeper into Amelia's core, her knuckles pressing against her with each stroke, adding a new dimension to the pleasure.

She came around Simone's fingers, her pussy spasming hard and her thighs shaking so much she had to use the couch back to hold herself up.

When the feeling subsided and she came back to herself, her heart was pounding and Simone came out from under the negligee with a grin. "What was that about tying me up and having your way with me?"

"Oh, we still have time for that," Amelia said. She pulled the nightie over her head and looped the thin shoulder straps around Simone's wrists. "Sit."

She ordered her onto the couch, then pulled Simone's hands over her head, turning the negligee into a makeshift silk handkerchief to tie her to the wooden arm of the couch. She straddled Simone's chest while she worked, teasing her with the sight of her glistening, still throbbing sex.

Then she crawled down to the other end of the couch and unbuttoned Simone's pants. "Your turn."

---

*A*melia and Simone didn't have a conventional type of relationship. Her availability was one of the reasons Amelia had resisted dating for so long, and Simone's schedule was just as hectic as her own. There were a lot of reasons for things not to work out between them, but they both wanted them to. They wanted to make time to see each other, and make the most of their time together.

And so it worked.

In fact, Simone was the best thing that had ever happened to Amelia, and she knew after just three months together that she never wanted another woman as long as she lived. Simone was it for her, and she was everything.

On their three-month anniversary, they made sure that their schedules aligned. They spent a romantic day in at Amelia's house, where they tended to gravitate more than Simone's apartment because it was larger and the coffee was better. Amelia had been thinking lately of asking Simone to let her lease go and move in with her. It was fast, but Simone had moved fast when she told Amelia that she loved her—and Amelia was so glad she had.

She decided she would ask when the moment felt right. Maybe tonight, maybe someday soon.

They spent the day just relaxing together. They stayed in bed all morning and made a lazy breakfast in the kitchen. They snuggled on the couch and watched the leaves fall outside Amelia's window. They took a bubble bath together in the afternoon and sipped on chilled wine in the tub. And in the evening, they had plans with friends.

While they got ready, Amelia asked, "Are you sure this is how you want to spend our anniversary?"

Simone wrapped her in a big hug from behind, telling her, "All I want tonight—all I ever want—is to spend time with you. If I get to be with you, I don't care if there are a hundred people double-dating with us."

"Triple-dating," Amelia corrected her.

They were going to meet up with Kelsey, who Amelia had been mentoring more actively lately, and her girlfriend Zara, as well as Zara's best friend Mel and her girlfriend Court.

"That's not what I meant," Amelia said. "I meant going to a forensic investigation exhibit at the museum."

It was only in town for a few weeks, and everyone in Amelia's professional circles had been talking about it. She had to see it, but with her crazy schedule and Simone's, tonight was the only night they could go.

Simone turned Amelia around in her arms so they were facing each other. She had a big grin on her face. "Okay, if you feel like it's unfair to 'drag' me to this exhibit, then this is what we'll do: the museum is for you, so when we're done, we'll do something for me."

The glimmer in her eyes made Amelia's core tighten. "And what would that be?"

"Guess."

The museum was crowded, and the exhibit was everything Amelia's colleagues said it was. She and Simone wandered through it, talking to their friends and looking at artifacts and subtly flirting with each other. They talked about the exhibit and also about mundane things like how their days had gone.

"I had my quarterly performance review today," Simone said after a while. "And the probies are officially not probies anymore."

"Good for them," Amelia said. "They all passed?"

"Yeah, surprisingly," Simone chuckled. "Even Larson. They'll be reassigned to whatever firehouses need them, although I think I'm going to try to keep Velez. I like watching you mentor Kelsey and I bet I could be a good influence for Velez. She reminds me of when I was a newly minted firefighter."

"I'm sure you'd make a great mentor," Amelia said, beaming with pride. "So I take it your performance review was positive?"

"Yeah, it was," Simone said. She was smiling in a way that told Amelia she was holding something back, and she nudged Simone's ribs.

"What?"

"The fire chief told me I can start training to be a captain as soon as there's an opening," she said, practically bursting with the news.

Amelia stopped in her tracks, her jaw dropping. "You held onto that news *all day*? That's amazing!"

"I didn't want to steal the limelight," Simone explained. "It's our anniversary so today should be about us."

"Whatever happens to one of us affects us both now that we're a couple," Amelia pointed out. "And I want to celebrate with you. Don't keep good news from me!"

"Okay, I'm sorry," Simone laughed.

"What's going on?" Zara asked as their paths crossed.

"Simone's going to be a fire captain!" Amelia said. Mel brought Court over and they all congratulated her.

"That's wonderful," Kelsey said. "Fox County is lucky to have you."

"They're lucky to have all of us," Court chimed in. "We're badass women."

They all agreed on that point, and then slowly the couples broke apart again, each going their own way. Amelia pulled Simone to the side so they weren't blocking any exhibits, and then she took Simone's hands.

"I love you so much."

"I love you too," Simone answered.

"I want you to move in with me," Amelia said. Apparently, this was the moment. Ultimately, there was only the present—and Simone had been teaching Amelia to live in the now ever since they met. "I don't want to be apart from you any more than I have to be," she continued. "And if you don't want to move into my place, if you'd rather we find someplace we can build a home in together—"

Simone cut her off with a kiss. "I would love to move in with you, Amelia."

"Really?"

"Yes," she said. "I don't care where we live, as long as I get to wake up next to your beautiful face every morning. Well, as much as our schedules allow."

Amelia laughed. "We'll make it happen."

"Yes, we will," Simone agreed. "Because when you

find your soulmate, there's no amount of effort that's too much if it means you get to be with her. Happy anniversary, Amelia."

"Happy anniversary," she repeated, squeezing Simone's hand tight, never letting go.

EPILOGUE
CLARK

*W*ell, this really wasn't ideal.

He'd been Mark Davis for over two months and he'd signed up for a rideshare service he'd never used before, just to make sure his tracks were well-covered. He'd had to jump through a few extra security hoops now that everyone was on edge, but his ID was solid and he knew how to get his hands on a valid Social Security number.

The problem was that his last failed friend had become somewhat of a celebrity. She'd started off on the twelve o'clock news, but her story picked up a surprising amount of steam and by now, she'd gone on pretty much every local news channel and a few of the national ones. With her talking about rideshare stranger danger all over the place, women weren't ordering rides anymore. And they sure as hell weren't ordering them from early-30s white men like him... was it his fault that he fit the major demographic for pretty much every violent crime in America?

He should probably count himself lucky that the police sketch they eventually released to the media didn't look like anyone in particular. It was just a generic Caucasian male. Whether that was because the girl hadn't gotten a close enough look at him or because Clark actually *was* generic, he didn't know.

Right now, he didn't care. He had bigger problems than digging into what was wrong with him in his core.

He had no money, his landlord was on his ass—as if it were a privilege to live in the cockroach-infested studio apartment Clark called home—and on top of that, he was lonely.

Critically so.

For the last few weeks, none of the passengers he'd managed to pick up wanted to talk to him—at least not any of the ones he thought had friend potential. They were all defensive, or they traveled in groups and talked only to each other, or they clutched pepper spray keychains the whole time they were in his car. Clark hadn't had a full conversation with anyone but his land-lord in nearly a month, and that had only been about how much he owed. It was starting to make him a little crazy.

Crazy enough and lonely enough to do something he hadn't done in five years.

He got in his new-to-him car and drove three and a half hours to the State Correctional Institution in Muncy. He signed in, walked through the metal detector, and got a visitor's badge. And then he went into the visitation room and sat down at a round table, in a slightly wobbly old chair like the ones he remembered from grade school. And he waited for his mother to appear.

When she saw him, she looked surprised. He'd been on her visitors list since she went in, but it had been years since he last came to see her.

When he saw her, he couldn't believe how fragile and old she appeared after six years in prison. That was six of a possible twenty-five. She was eligible for parole in four more years, but if she didn't get it, he wasn't sure she would survive to the end of her sentence. Not from the looks of her.

She sat down across from him. Didn't even try to hug him or shake his hand. He knew from long-ago visits that the guards wouldn't allow it, but he'd hoped that she would at least try, after five years of estrangement.

"What are you doing here?" she asked.

"I missed you."

"Bullshit," she said. She glanced at the vending machines lining one wall of the visitation room. "Could you get me a soda before you ask for whatever it is you want?"

Clark's heart, what was left of it, shriveled and cracked in his chest. His own mother wasn't happy to see him, and with one sentence, she'd reduced this entire visit to a transaction.

Well, she was a counterfeiter after all. Currency was all she ever cared about.

Clark went to the vending machines. Twelve-ounce cans cost a dollar-fifty, absolute price gouging. He had a bunch of quarters in his pocket that he'd been planning to use on the toll roads, but he bought his mother a soda, then got himself one too. He'd have to take the back roads home because those quarters were the only cash he had on him.

He carried the sodas back to the table and watched his mother chug half of hers in one long swallow. When she was finally done guzzling, she said, "They pay me nineteen cents an hour to wash sheets. Do you know how long it's been since I could afford a soda?"

A thank you would have been nice, Clark thought instead of answering.

She went back to drinking, then belched loudly when she reached the bottom of the can. She set it aside and asked, "So, what are you here for?"

"I wanted to see how you were," Clark said.

She narrowed her eyes at him.

"And I was wondering how your appeals were going."

"I ran out of those," she said. "You know that."

They sat in silence for a moment or two, taking each other's measure, and at last, he said quietly, "I need money, Mom."

She sat back, crossed her arms over her chest, and looked supremely satisfied at having made him ask. When in her life had she ever done anything without making him beg first? Clark couldn't think of a single instance.

"Well, in that case, you came to the right person," she said. She couldn't resist salting his wound, adding,

"Although I'm disappointed you even need to ask. How many times did you help me when you were younger?"

It was all he did, other than go to school so CPS wouldn't notice anything out of place. But she'd never taught him the entire counterfeiting process. She always needed him to be dependent on her—and she never trusted him not to screw it up.

"Okay, let's get started," she said, reaching across the table and swiping the second soda can.

Clark didn't even complain when she started drinking his Pepsi. She was actually going to take him into her confidence, and that was worth far more than his toll road money. Despite all the time he'd spent trying to distance himself from her in the last five years, he found himself basking in Mommy's attention.

For the rest of the visiting hour, even though they were just whispering counterfeiting steps, he felt loved. Wanted. Seen.

And when he walked out of that prison full of new information, he had a plan—a future, a way to hold onto those feelings all the time.

He was going to pay his rent, get some decent food for the first time all month, and then he was going to get out there and make some new friends... even if he had to pay for them.

A NOTE FROM CARA

Hello!

Thank you so much for reading *Dark Skies* – I hope you enjoyed it!

If you'd like to be notified when I publish a new book, sign up to my newsletter at https://bit.ly/2LPRHXI - I send out a monthly email packed with **free short stories, behind-the-scenes details into my works in progress and all kinds of fun stuff.**

You can also connect with me on social media using the icons below.

With love,

Cara

facebook.com/caramalonebooks

twitter.com/caramalonebooks

goodreads.com/caramalonebooks

bookbub.com/authors/cara-malone

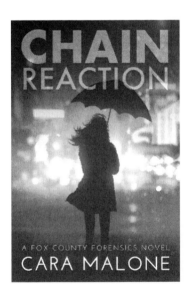

*a*dark green Camry pulled up to the curb and
Dylan bent over at the passenger door, checking
the driver's face against the photo on her rideshare app.

There'd been a near-abduction in Fox City just a few

weeks ago, and while Dylan herself wasn't all that concerned with stranger danger, her parents had been freaking the eff out, to put it in the parlance of the times.

"I don't know why you don't drive your own car all the time!" her mother had said when she found out Dylan still used the apps.

"I do most of the time, Mom. There are just certain situations where rideshare is better," she'd said. Situations like tonight, when she was going out to meet some friends at a pub and she didn't want to worry about how many beers she could have or whether her car would get towed if she left it in the lot overnight.

"Better than getting murdered?" her mom had shot back, not missing a beat.

Her dad had even offered to buy her a brand-new car, thinking maybe that the Little Beetle That Could, which she'd been driving since college, was the problem.

"Dad, I'm thirty-two," she'd reminded him. "I have a good job -- if I need a new car, I can buy it for myself."

Her mother had just smirked at that. Even after ten years with the coroner's office, Dylan still couldn't convince them that her job as a chemist was more lab work than anything else. She was sure they both pictured her elbow-deep in body cavities all day, instead of in her fluorescently lit lab with its whirring centrifuges and more test tubes than you can shake a stick at.

They worried, and as their only daughter, Dylan could sort of understand why.

But hey, she was their only *daughter*, not their only child, after all. She had three older brothers and sometimes it'd be nice if they shouldered some of the parental anxiety for a change.

Since there was a slim chance of that happening, Dylan at least tried to meet her folks half-way. She took her chances with rideshare drivers, but she made sure she was getting in the right car and she always told her friends when to expect her. Plus, she boxed in her free time. Just let a would-be kidnapper mess with her.

"Hey," she said as she slid into the back seat of the Camry. "I'm Dylan. Thanks for the ride."

"I'm Mark," her driver said, twisting around in his seat and holding his hand out. He looked around Dylan's age, maybe a few years younger, even, but aged by a receding hairline. He looked like his profile picture, though, and that was all Dylan really cared about where his looks were concerned.

"Going to the Taphouse, huh?" he said as he pulled away from the curb. "Meeting friends?"

"Yeah," Dylan answered. In fact, she was texting one of them, Elise, right now so her attention was divided.

We're all here, Elise was saying. *Got a table in the back.*

Dylan was meeting a group of coworkers for end-of-the-week drinks. They'd done it a handful of times and had fun, but the fact that it had become a weekly ritual was entirely down to Elise and her persistent planning efforts.

In the car now, Dylan texted back. *Be there in ten.*

"Isn't that a cop bar?" the driver asked.

"Umm, it might be," Dylan said. It was right downtown, about halfway between the precinct and the medical examiner's office where she worked, so it was safe to say you ran into a fair number of officers there. "I'm not a cop, though."

"Oh yeah?" He looked at her in the rearview mirror, and her belly turned to ice.

Why? His eyes were on the road again and he was just making friendly conversation. Dylan had been leered at before, and that wasn't what this guy was doing. Was she letting her parents' stranger danger fears get to her?

"What do you do?" he asked.

She tried to shake it off. "I'm a chemist."

"Oh, that's neat. So you work Monday to Friday, I bet."

Nope, this guy was definitely freaking her out. What was he doing, trying to figure out when people would notice she was missing? Or planning to pop by her office? She was glad she hadn't actually told him where she worked.

When in doubt, just get out, her mom's advice floated through her head.

The odds that she was overreacting were high, but if she got out now, she only had about eight blocks to walk to the Taphouse, or she could call a different rideshare driver. One who didn't give her the willies.

"You know what?" she said casually. "I just saw one of my friends on the sidewalk back there. Can you let me out?"

"Where?" He made no move to slow down, looking into his rearview mirror instead.

"Oh, about half a block back," Dylan said. Fortunately, it was a Friday night and there were people walking downtown to cover her lie.

Unfortunately, Mark was giving absolutely no indication that he planned to pull over. And even worse, when Dylan looked at her door for the first time since getting into the car, she realized it was an old car with a manual lock, and the plunger was missing.

You're locked in, her brain was screaming in her mother's voice.

Her eyes must have been wide and panicked when she locked onto Mark's gaze in the rearview mirror again, but he didn't seem to notice her terror. He just smiled benignly back at her and said, "I'm really not supposed to change course -- I could get docked for it."

Dylan had no clue whether that was true or not. Her brain was hardly processing his words at all because the only thing she was thinking was that the last girl some sick fuck -- maybe this very sick fuck -- had attempted to abduct had escaped. She didn't have the benefit of a tornado for a distraction, but she did have a hell of a lot of fight in her.

Like when the girls on the playground talked behind her back because she used to prefer the sports the boys were playing.

Like when those very same boys picked on her and called her names -- tomboy was the nicest of them -- because she was a kid without a country.

Like when she was interviewing for her job and it

came down to herself and some cis white guy fresh out of college who knew people high-up in the county.

Dylan didn't let people shove her into predetermined boxes when she was younger, she didn't let them take what was rightfully hers when she was older, and she sure as hell wasn't going to let some freak of a rideshare driver take what he wanted now.

Whatever the hell that was.

"Do you like Bob Dylan? Or maybe your parents did?" he was saying now. It was such a complete one-eighty from the last time he spoke that Dylan felt whiplashed.

"What?"

"Your name."

Yeah, I got that part... as if you're the first person to ask, she thought, but she knew better than to antagonize the guy.

"*Why?*" was all she managed.

"Just making conversation," he said. "Getting to know you."

"I don't want to know you, I want to get out of the car," she snapped. Okay, so much for not being antagonistic.

"We'll be there shortly," he said, that same serene, stupid smile on his face. Only Dylan knew he wasn't talking about the Taphouse anymore. You didn't take all the locking mechanisms out of your doors if you had pure intentions.

Her pulse was pounding so fast she could hear it in her ears. They were a couple blocks from the pub, and she knew she had to get out of the car before he could take her out of downtown. There was safety in numbers, and if she could make a scene of some sort, there was no way he could carry out whatever plans he had.

She reached for the old-fashioned handle to roll her window down and scream for help. She touched a flat door panel, with a tiny screw sticking out where the crank used to be. Of course he would remove those too.

Shit!

"My friends are expecting me," she said.

"Must be nice." His voice turned icy and so did the blood in her veins. Did she just strike a nerve? Okay, she'd officially had enough and she was getting out of this damn car by whatever means necessary. "Pull over now or I'm calling 911."

Mark scowled at her in the rearview. "Why would you do that?"

"Because I want out!"

The adrenaline was flowing freely now and Dylan was sure that if she didn't get out of this car in the next ten minutes, she would end up however that girl who was all over the news had been intended to wind up before that tornado intervened on her behalf.

She squeezed between the seats into the front of the car, pulling herself through the narrow space with no regard to whether she'd actually fit, or if it was safe while they were cruising down the road. There was no safety now -- only escape.

"Hey!" Mark cried. "Stop!"

Dylan already had her hand on the passenger door

handle. Thank God he'd only removed the locks in the back. She shoved the door open and did what little mental preparation she could for diving head-first out of a moving car. Then a hand closed around her ankle.

"Are you trying to get yourself killed?" Mark asked. He actually sounded *concerned* and, miraculously, the car started to slow.

Now or never.

Dylan mule-kicked as hard as she could with her free foot. The heel of her sneaker connected with something fleshy, and the hand disappeared from her other ankle.

"Fucking bitch!" Mark screamed and slammed on the brakes. Dylan didn't wait for a written invitation -- she scrambled out of the car, her palms hitting the rough asphalt before her feet touched solid ground. Then she ran as fast as she could to the only place she could think of -- the Taphouse, and Elise.

***

Inside the pub, it was dim and noisy. There were people crowded around every table and lined up at the bar, and Dylan's heart was still pounding. She wasn't sure if she was going to pass out, vomit, or cry. When she spotted her ME's Office friends at the table in the back Elise had texted her about, she felt entirely incapable of sitting down and chatting like nothing happened.

"Hey! We got you your usual IPA--" Kelsey, one of the investigators, said when she approached the table.

"I, uh, I'm going to the restroom," Dylan muttered, barely slowing down. She walked right past her friends, all of them looking confused, and made a beeline for the narrow hallway at the back of the pub.

The restroom was nothing to write home about -- a little dirty, dimly lit, but at least it was empty. Dylan went to one of the sinks and braced her hands on the edge of the counter. She was still trying to decide what bodily function would be the most effective way of expelling all the stress she'd just built up.

When she caught sight of her reflection in the mirror, she knew why her friends had looked so freaked out. She looked haunted, and sweat had matted her short, dark hair down on her temples.

She turned on the faucet, running the water as cold as it would go, then bent over and splashed her face a few times. It felt good, like a shock to bring her back to reality, and she rubbed the back of her neck too, to cool down.

Then she heard the restroom door creak open and she pulled her head up so fast she smacked her head on the faucet.

"Shit!" she hissed, only feeling the pain once she'd seen that it was Elise standing there, and not Mark the rideshare lunatic.

"Aww," Elise said, immediately crossing the small space and putting her hand lightly on the crown of Dylan's head. "You okay?"

"Yeah, I'm not bleeding, am I?" Dylan asked.

"No," Elise said after she'd checked. "That's not what I meant, though. Did something happen on the way over here?"

Suddenly, Dylan's body decided on that stress

release valve. It came in the form of tears -- no, full-on sobs. In an instant, she'd gone from calming herself down at the sink to bawling her eyes out, and her best friend didn't hesitate to pull her into her arms. It was entirely uncharacteristic of her. Dylan couldn't remember the last time she'd cried, and she was sure Elise had never witnessed it.

All the same, Elise wrapped her up in a warm, soft hug and ran her hand up and down Dylan's back. She laid Dylan's head on her shoulder and rested her cheek against it, and she just waited for the tears to subside.

She smelled like lavender, and for a petite girl, she was surprisingly easy to curl up against. Had they ever hugged before? Not this long. That was Dylan's first conscious thought when the waterworks stopped.

This is a line you do not need to cross. This time, the scolding voice inside her head was her own, speaking from experience. Elise was just comforting her, but her mind had gone somewhere else in that brief moment.

Dylan let go of her and turned back to the sink, splashing her face one more time to get rid of the redness. Then she turned the water off and while she dried her skin with a rough paper towel, she said, "You're going to be mad at me."

Elise frowned. "Why would I be mad?"

Dylan cringed. Her parents weren't the only ones who'd lectured her about rideshare apps lately.

Elise must have read the truth on her face because she put her fists on her hips and said, "You didn't! After what happened to that girl?" And then, a moment later as recognition dawned, she added, "Oh my God, did it happen to you too?"

"Almost," Dylan admitted.

And then Elise's arms were around her again, squeezing her so hard she couldn't take a breath. "Never, never, never again, damn it! I can't lose you!"

Read Chain Reaction on Amazon
Coming September 9, 2021

LESFIC BOOK CLUB

Calling all lesfic lovers!

Join us for a monthly book club, talk to your favorite lesfic authors, check out our growing community of published and aspiring writers, and hang out in daily chats with fellow lesfic lovers. Check out the group at http://tinyurl.com/lesficlove

Printed in Great Britain
by Amazon